D0650480

"I think you're the sexiest, most beautiful woman I've ever seen."

The truth came tumbling out of Mitch's mouth.

"But you wouldn't have called me. Why not?"

"You know why not."

"Because you work for Dad. Mitch, that's so silly. I don't care who you work for."

"You should."

"You'll never make the second move, either, will you?" She lifted a lock of hair from his forehead.

He clenched his jaw. "Be careful."

"I don't want to be careful, Mitch. Something hit me very hard the evening we met, and I want to find out what it is."

"If you keep touching me, you will," he warned.

"Don't be so damn noble," she whispered.

His resistance vanished. His mouth covered hers in a kiss of utter possession, without gentleness, without tenderness, conveying only the dark swirl of emotions he was feeling.

Its intensity took her breath. She raised her head, breaking the kiss.

"Maybe I *am* playing with fire with you," she whispered, and shaped a shaky smile.

Dear Reader,

Welcome to Silhouette Desire! This month, we have something special in store for you—book #1 of the *new* Silhouette miniseries, ALWAYS A BRIDESMAID! In ALWAYS A BRIDESMAID! you'll get to read how five women get the men of their dreams. Each book will be featured in a different Silhouette series...one book a month beginning this month with *The Engagement Party* by Barbara Boswell.

In addition, we've got a wonderful MAN OF THE MONTH by award-winning author Jennifer Greene called *Single Dad.* Josh is a hero you'll never forget.

Don't miss *Dr. Daddy,* book #3 in Elizabeth Bevarly's series FROM HERE TO MATERNITY. And a new series, WEDDING BELLES, by Carole Buck launches with the charming *Annie Says I Do.*

A book by Jackie Merritt is always a treat, and she's sure to win new fans—and please her present admirers— with *Hesitant Husband.* And Anne Marie Winston's *Rancher's Wife* completes what I feel is a perfect month!

Silhouette Desire—you've just got to read them all!

Enjoy!

Lucia Macro
Senior Editor

Please address questions and book requests to:
Silhouette Reader Service
U.S.: 3010 Walden Ave., P.O. Box 1325, Buffalo, NY 14269
Canadian: P.O. Box 609, Fort Erie, Ont. L2A 5X3

JACKIE MERRITT
HESITANT HUSBAND

SILHOUETTE *Desire*®
Published by Silhouette Books
America's Publisher of Contemporary Romance

If you purchased this book without a cover you should be aware
that this book is stolen property. It was reported as "unsold and
destroyed" to the publisher, and neither the author nor the
publisher has received any payment for this "stripped book."

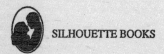 SILHOUETTE BOOKS

ISBN 0-373-05935-3

HESITANT HUSBAND

Copyright © 1995 by Carolyn Joyner

All rights reserved. Except for use in any review, the reproduction
or utilization of this work in whole or in part in any form by any
electronic, mechanical or other means, now known or hereafter
invented, including xerography, photocopying and recording, or in
any information storage or retrieval system, is forbidden without
the written permission of the editorial office, Silhouette Books,
300 East 42nd Street, New York, NY 10017 U.S.A.

All characters in this book have no existence outside the imagination of
the author and have no relation whatsoever to anyone bearing the same
name or names. They are not even distantly inspired by any individual
known or unknown to the author, and all incidents are pure invention.

This edition published by arrangement with Harlequin Enterprises B.V.

® and TM are trademarks of Harlequin Enterprises B.V., used under
license. Trademarks indicated with ® are registered in the United States
Patent and Trademark Office, the Canadian Trade Marks Office and in
other countries.

Printed in U.S.A.

Books by Jackie Merritt

JACKIE MERRITT

and her husband live just outside of Las Vegas, Nevada. An accountant for many years, Jackie has happily traded numbers for words. Next to family, books are her greatest joy. She started writing in 1987 and her efforts paid off in 1988 with the publication of her first novel. When she's not writing or enjoying a good book, Jackie dabbles in watercolor painting and likes playing the piano in her spare time.

One

The Armstrong home had Mitch gaping.

With his pickup idling, he checked the address Sarge Armstrong had written down for him against the brass numbers on the brick and wrought-iron fencing. He was at the right address, and he probably should have expected his boss's home to look like this. Within the fence the property was a good five acres of velvety grass, stately old trees with the pale tender leaves of spring, budding flower beds and an immense brick house with mullioned windows, exuding solidity, comfort and the kind of wealth Mitch Conover could only imagine. Until this moment Sarge's dinner invitation hadn't made him at all nervous; now he wondered if his casual slacks, shirt and shoes were appropriate.

Drawing a breath, Mitch cautiously pulled into the long driveway. It curved along the front of the house, and he debated on precisely which section of the impressive drive he should park. His pickup truck belonged at the back of the house, not at the front, he thought wryly. Wherever the hired help parked.

Hired help or not, he was an invited guest. After handing him a promotion today, Sarge had slapped him on the back, shaken his hand and said in a very friendly way, "I'd like you to come to dinner this evening, Mitch. If you don't have prior plans, that is. It won't be formal or crowded, just Mrs. Armstrong, you and me. How about it?"

"No prior plans, sir," Mitch had responded, so pleased with his official promotion to project supervisor that he would have canceled anything else to accept Sarge Armstrong's invitation. Even without the promotion he would have been elated over a dinner invitation from the boss. There were a few sour apples in Sarge's company, Armstrong Paving and Asphalt, but for the most part Mitch's co-workers liked and respected their employer.

But he still hadn't expected to be entertained in a home of this quality. Actually, he had arrived with few expectations, just a personal elation because of the compliment Sarge had paid him by inviting him to his home. Being singled out by the boss, being noticed, was exciting, and seemed like proof to Mitch that he was indeed advancing in the company.

Before getting out, Mitch did a rare thing: he took a look at himself in the rearview mirror. He was almost thirty years old, tall, muscular and in excellent physical condition. Today his dark hair was as subdued as he could make it, and his jaw was almost shiny from the close shave he'd administered not more than an hour ago. He didn't stop to wonder if his face was attractive, as his own looks never entered his mind. Neither had his wardrobe until this minute. Ordinarily he never questioned his confidence, and finding himself doing so was disconcerting. Frowning, he opened the door of his truck and stepped out.

Sarge, himself, answered the doorbell. Wearing a big grin, he offered his hand. "Glad you could come, Mitch. Have any trouble finding the place?"

"No trouble, sir."

"None of that 'sir' stuff tonight, Mitch. Come on in. Sara's in the kitchen right now, but she'll be joining us in the den."

Sarge's clothing was slacks and a polo shirt, similar to the way Mitch was dressed. The older man led the way to a striking room with overstuffed chairs and sofa, wood-paneled walls, deep-pile carpeting and numerous wall shelves laden with books.

"Sit down, Mitch. Would you like a drink?"

Mitch cleared his throat, uncertain about answering that question until Sarge added, "I'm going to have a Scotch and water. There's beer, if you prefer, and soft drinks. Name your poison."

Relaxing, Mitch smiled. "I'll have a beer, thanks."

Sarge served the drinks and they sat in large, comfortable chairs in front of the fireplace "Your home is beautiful, Sarge," Mitch said.

"Sara and I like it. We bought it about fifteen years ago. It was badly run down and Sara had a fine old time refurbishing it. Oh, here's Sara now." Sarge stood up and Mitch bolted to his feet. "Honey, this is Mitch Conover. Mitch, my wife, Sara."

Sara Armstrong smiled warmly and walked over to Mitch to shake hands. "Very nice meeting you, Mitch."

"Nice meeting you, Mrs. Armstrong."

"Sara," she said firmly while moving to the sofa. Everyone sat down. "Dinner will be ready in about twenty minutes. Sarge tells me you're from Montana, Mitch."

"Yes, ma'am. A little town called Houghton." Sipping from his glass of beer, Mitch took note of Sara Armstrong's stylish clothes and hairdo. She was a small, chic, slender woman who appeared years younger than her husband, though Mitch wondered if that wasn't because Sarge had rugged, rough-hewn features and Sara's were delicate and very feminine.

"I've been to Houghton," Sara said. "About two years ago, wasn't it, Sarge?"

"About that," Sarge replied. "That's when Mitch started working for the company, Sara. We had a paving contract for a twenty-mile stretch of highway just outside of town, and one of our mechanics quit." Sarge smiled. "Mitch came along and applied for a job at just the right moment."

"But you're not a mechanic anymore, are you?" Sara inquired of Mitch.

"No, ma'am."

"He's a project supervisor now, Sara. One of the best," Sarge announced. "Don't be embarrassed, Mitch. It's the truth. You've earned your promotions, and I see a bright future for you with the company."

"Thank you, sir."

Sarge chuckled. "A little intimidated by the boss, though, I can see. Well, you'll get over that."

Mitch wondered about that. Sarge Armstrong was a commanding figure, and in her own way so was his wife. These were people who were completely certain of their place in the world, accustomed to living graciously and being comfortable with wealth. He might attain their status some day, though it couldn't possibly happen for a good many years. In the meantime, he was an employee and glad to have a steady, satisfying job with an aggressive, upwardly mobile company.

"You're not married?" Sara said questioningly to Mitch.

He gave his head a shake. "Never been married, ma'am."

Sara smiled. "But there must be someone important somewhere. Maybe in Montana?"

"No, ma'am." Mitch was trying hard to relax and only partially succeeding. For one thing, he couldn't quite bring himself to address Mrs. Armstrong by her given name. Maybe in time, he thought. Should the opportunity to do so ever arise, that is, as it wasn't likely that he and the Armstrongs would see much of each other socially.

"Mitch spends his free time building up his education, Sara," Sarge told his wife. "What are you taking, Mitch, two classes?"

"Right now I'm enrolled in an advanced business course and another in the basics of structural engineering," Mitch replied. "They take up most of my evenings."

"Well, that's very commendable," Sara exclaimed. "No wonder you're going places in the company."

"Kim!" Sarge got up from his chair. "Come on in, honey."

Mitch turned his head to see whom Sarge was speaking to, and immediately suffered a jolt to his nervous system. A young dark-haired woman was entering the room, smiling at everyone, including himself, and going over to Sarge to plant a kiss on his cheek. "Hi, Dad."

She moved to Sara and bent over to kiss her mother's cheek. "Hello, Mother."

"What a nice surprise." Sara was obviously happy to see her daughter. "Sit down and join us. Dinner will be ready soon. You can eat with us."

"Thanks, but I only stopped by to pick up a bolt of fabric. I can't stay but a minute."

"Kim, say hello to Mitch Conover," Sarge said. "Mitch, this is my daughter, Kimberly Armstrong."

Kim turned and smiled. "Hello, Mitch."

He had gotten up and was standing by his chair. Looking into Kim Armstrong's dancing violet eyes was like receiving a blow to the solar plexus. She was gorgeous, beautiful, sexy and sensual, the most stunningly exciting woman he'd ever seen. "Hello, Miss Armstrong."

For some reason she laughed, and the husky sound seemed to pierce Mitch's skin and careen around in his body like something lost and searching. He was staring and couldn't stop himself.

"Please call me Kim," she told him.

He was still staring. "Whatever you say." What was difficult to digest was that Kim, too, seemed to be staring. At him. Could that be? Could she be as dumbfounded as he felt?

"You can sit down for a minute, can't you?" Sara said to her daughter in a cajoling manner.

Kim tore her gaze from Mitch Conover. "I really can't, Mother. I have an appointment." She looked at Mitch again. "Are you an old friend, or what?"

Mitch felt a rush of blood to his face. Her question undeniably expressed interest, and apparently her parents being present didn't bother her in the least.

Their presence bothered him, though. "I work for your father," he said with some coolness. His giddiness was passing, thank God. Admiring his boss's daughter right in front of the man was imposing on Sarge's hospitality a bit too much.

"Oh, I see," Kim murmured, taken aback by Mitch's distant tone. Obviously she shouldn't have let her admiration get in the way of good manners, but something about the man had chased everything else from her mind.

Mitch's stomach sank. Kim's *I see* said it all. He was an employee, a peon, a nothing in her world. Almost belligerently he squared his shoulders.

"Kim's an interior decorator," Sarge said with unmistakable pride. "A very successful decorator, I might add."

Mitch had nothing to say to an interior decorator. He'd never even met an interior decorator before.

"Yes, well, this decorator has an appointment in..." Kim glanced at her watch "...fifteen minutes. I've got to run. It was nice meeting you, Mitch."

He nodded. "Nice meeting you."

"Bye, Dad...Mother. See you soon." Kim left with a feeling of perplexity. Maybe Mitch was attached and not interested. Maybe she had only imagined that simmering look passing between them. But...had she ever run into a better-looking guy? Or one who'd immediately rocked her very foundation? Touched her inner self so intimately?

Sarge sat down and picked up his drink. "Kim still uses a room behind the garage to store materials. She dashes in and out all the time to get something she needs."

"Indeed, she does," Sara put in with a laugh. "When she first started in the business, Sarge fixed up that room for her to work out of. She orders upholstery and drapery materials from all over the world, and there are dozens of bolts of the most exquisite fabric out there."

Mitch gingerly returned to his chair. "Do you have other children?"

"Just Kim," Sara said fondly. "How about you, Mitch? Do you have family in Montana?"

"A sister. And a brother-in-law," he added after a moment. "Blair got married last fall. We still own my mother's home in Houghton. We're renting it out."

"Always nice to have extra income," Sarge commented with a chuckle.

A woman came in. "Dinner is ready, Mrs. Armstrong."

"Thank you, Lois." Sara got up. "Are you two gentlemen ready for dinner?"

"All set, honey," Sarge exclaimed. "Come on, Mitch. We've got the best darned cook in the Northwest. I'm sure you'll enjoy dinner."

Mitch couldn't get Kim Armstrong out of his mind. He went to work during the day and to his classes in the evening, and no matter how busy he was, Kim Armstrong remained behind nearly every thought and activity. This was the first time a woman had made that sort of impact on him. He thought of her rich dark hair and recalled that it had been knotted in a loose bun at the back of her head. So, was it long when it wasn't trussed up that way? Her eyes were violet, he remembered. Truly violet. He'd never seen eyes that color before. Her laugh had been the most sensual sound he'd ever heard, and her smile was a haunting memory.

Often he tried to stop himself from dredging up every tiny detail of their meeting. Something unusual had passed between them, but it meant nothing. How could it? Kim was the boss's daughter, an interior decorator, a woman who traveled in circles that he would probably never get near. Even her memory made him feel clumsy and gauche, and no one else he'd ever known had caused that discomfiting sensation.

It wasn't anything to worry about, he told himself. It wasn't likely that he and Kim Armstrong would ever see each other again. What possible occasion could bring them together? As nice as Sarge was being to him, the man wasn't apt to invite him to hang around his house, which Mitch wouldn't do in any case. But where else would he run into Kim when he didn't even have the slightest idea about which section of Seattle she lived in?

About two weeks after meeting Kim, Mitch picked up his mail, as usual, on his way into his apartment building. Carrying his lunch pail and the small stack of mail, he unlocked his apartment door, dropped everything on a table and sat down to take off his boots. His mind was on the test scheduled for this evening's business class, and it was only after remembering that his sister owed him a letter that he reached for the mail.

Most of it was advertisements and slated for the trash can, and there was nothing from Blair. But one envelope stopped him. Frowning at the handwritten name and address—*his* name and address—and at the return address—a company by the name of Meridian Homes—he finally tore the envelope open and extracted an engraved invitation.

Meridian Homes announces the opening of five exciting new models at 3135 Northwest Lakeview Avenue. You are cordially invited to attend the official opening at 1:00 p.m. on Saturday the fifth of June. Refreshments will be served.

Mitch looked at the envelope again. It had been specifically addressed to him, but why would a developer single him out like this? Then, on the lower left-hand corner of the invitation he saw: Models decorated by Kimberly Armstrong.

His mouth dropped open. This invitation was Kim's doing! His heart began beating a mile a minute. Why would she go out of her way to include him in what was obviously a formal affair? Dare he believe she wanted to see him again?

Mitch got up to pace in his stocking feet, with his mouth dry and his stomach churning. This was startling, incredible. She must want to see him again, but why? Was it possible that she was having as much trouble forgetting him as he was having with her? But didn't she understand that they were poles apart? He worked for her father, for Pete's sake, and she . . . she . . .

She was a princess, a stunningly beautiful woman who was used to the very best life had to offer. Her every whim had probably been indulged by Sarge and Sara since her birth. It was a wonder she worked at all, albeit at a classy profession like interior decorating.

Mitch gathered up the junk mail and the invitation and stuffed the works in the trash. He wouldn't go to that opening. Deluding himself that he had a chance with Kim Armstrong would be the silliest thing he'd ever done. He was a man with both feet on the ground, and Kim might think one startling look between a man and a woman meant something, but he knew better. He'd grown up poor. His father had died when he was just a kid, and his mother, sister and himself had struggled to make ends meet from then on. So be it. One couldn't change history, but one could sure as hell do something about the future. And if hard work, dedication and a gnawing ambition to better himself added up to anything, he would someday be a success. Until then, he would study and learn and not waste time dreaming about an unattainable woman.

After showering and eating, Mitch left to attend his class and take that test. When it was over, he felt he'd done all right, and he stopped at a market on the way home to buy a six-pack of beer.

In his apartment again, he opened one of the beers and sat in his minuscule living room to drink it. Kim's image was immediately with him. He closed his eyes and relived their meeting. If she wasn't Sarge's daughter he would already have found a way to see her again.

His eyes jerked open. This was getting ridiculous. Mooning over a woman he could never have was adolescent foolishness, and he had better things to do with his time.

But... that invitation remained intriguing, and Mitch couldn't forget it however hard he tried. The fact that Kim was thinking about him had his gut in a turmoil. What did she hope would happen if he attended that opening? What did she want to happen? The possibilities made his mouth go dry in spite of the cold beer he was drinking.

Deliberately he concentrated on the modest little apartment, telling himself that this was his world, three small rooms and a bath, a far cry from what Kim Armstrong was accustomed to. He smirked slightly. Envisioning her walking through these rooms and trying to find something redeeming in the plain furnishings and nearly bare walls was funny.

Almost funny. Envisioning Kim Armstrong here led to fantasies that weren't at all humorous, fantasies that made him break out in a sweat.

"That's enough," he muttered aloud, and got up to toss down the rest of his beer and go to bed. Carrying the empty bottle to the kitchen for disposal, he stared broodingly into the trash can. The Meridian Homes invitation lay on top. Attending that opening would be the most inane thing he'd ever done.

She had violet eyes. He could almost see them. With a lunge he rescued the invitation and dropped the beer bottle into the can. Maybe he would attend the opening, maybe he wouldn't.

But he felt better with the invitation lying on the table, instead of mixing with the trash in that can. Snapping off the lights, he went to bed.

The opening was a huge success. Kim had shaken so many hands and received so many compliments on the decor of the model homes, her head was spinning. The crowd was beginning to thin out, though there were groups still standing around and talking, some of them holding drinks and tiny plates of hors d'oeuvres.

Despite the enormous success of the affair, Kim's spirit reeked with disappointment. No one knew it, of course. Her smiles were genuine, her conversation bright and cheerful. But Mitch Conover hadn't made an appearance, and she'd been so hopeful that he would.

Decorating five beautiful homes from the bare walls to the finished product had been an exciting project for Kim. Along with a number of private homes with various orders for redecorating, she had been on the go for months working on the models. Most of the winter, actually. It was over now and things would pretty much get back to normal, though she could already see that her business was going to increase because of these models. That was fine with her. Kim liked staying busy, a trait she had inherited from her father. The only time Sarge Armstrong became restless was when he wasn't bogged down with a dozen different demands on his time, and Kim viewed herself as being very much the same.

She stood now to one side, a little weary, a trifle strained. About two hundred people had trooped through the models and she was glad the affair was winding down. Her job here was over. From now on the success of the Meridian project would be up to the sales staff.

Sighing silently, she started for the cupboard in which she had left her purse. Halfway across the room she glanced at the door. Mitch Conover was standing there, looking uncomfortable, frowning in at the groups of people. His good looks and aura arrowed directly to the core of her.

Quickly Kim changed directions. She saw the look on Mitch's face the moment he spotted her coming, and her heart skipped a very noticeable beat.

"Hello, Mitch," she said a trifle breathlessly. "I didn't think you were coming."

Exactly as had happened at their first meeting, Mitch got that just-punched feeling. She was so pretty, so alive, and he wanted to stand there and just look at her. "Hello, Kim."

He managed a crooked grin. "I wasn't sure that invitation wasn't some kind of mistake."

"It wasn't a mistake. I put your name on the list myself."

"Figured as much. After I thought about it." He kept looking into her amazing eyes and then breaking the contact. He shouldn't be here. Why had he come? She was wearing a royal blue business suit, very chic, obviously expensive, and high, high heels. Her hair was down, kissing her shoulders and drawn back from the left side of her face by a glittering blue comb. For a second he looked at her lips, but the ensuing wave of heat in his body was much too discomfiting and he instantly looked elsewhere. "Did you have a good turnout?"

"Very good. More than two hundred guests. May I get you something? There are drinks and canapés..."

"Nothing, thanks. I only dropped by for a minute."

"Oh." Kim searched her brain for a way to keep him from running off. "Maybe you'd like to see the models. They're empty now. Most of the guests have gone." She smiled. "I'd like you to see my work."

He nearly asked her why. Her interest was again obvious, and it both bewildered and elated him. She shouldn't be interested in one of her father's employees. She shouldn't be standing there with that glorious smile and those luscious lips and letting him know she was interested. She shouldn't... he shouldn't...

"Yes," he said softly. "I'd like to see your work."

"Come this way."

Feeling a little punch-drunk, Mitch followed her through the room and out another door. The area was beautifully landscaped. There were sidewalks, and signs in front of each model home designating square footage and a name.

"This is the Chablis model," Kim said, preceding him up the walk. "It's the smallest of the units."

The exterior of the house was great, but the interior stunned Mitch. He looked at the light, airy colors, the wall treatments, the furnishings down to knickknacks and area rugs, the rich carpeting and tile, and could only say, "It's beautiful, Kim. You did it all?"

"Guilty as charged," Kim admitted with a smile. "Each home is decorated differently. My favorite is... No, I won't tell you. Let's see which one you like best."

They moved from model to model. Each was fabulous in its own way. After inspecting the fifth house, Kim asked, "Which one do you prefer?"

"That's a tough question. I like them all, but... I guess I like the Cabernet best."

Clapping her hands, Kim emitted a merry little laugh. "That's my favorite, too!"

"Are they named after wines, or am I missing something?"

"You're right on the mark, Mitch. I didn't name them. The Meridian people did that, but I don't dislike the names, do you?"

He grinned. She was so pretty and bright-eyed, and she made him feel good. "You really enjoy your work, don't you?"

"I love my work. Everyone should be so lucky." Her voice dropped and softened. "I'm glad you came, Mitch."

His grin faded. They were standing just outside of the fifth model, quite alone. Easily he could reach out and touch her, and a desire to do so created an ache in his gut. "Kim... this can't go anywhere."

Her eyes remained steady and probing his. It was such a naked statement, so blunt and fundamental, and she couldn't pretend to misunderstand. "I'm completely free. Are you?"

"That's not the point."

"That's precisely the point. I felt something strong and very potent the day we met. I still feel it. If you don't..."

"Don't say that." Turning his head, Mitch stared off into the distance. He was going to rue coming here. He already did. What man was strong enough to resist a woman like Kim? A woman who possessed not only beauty and brains, but a direct, open honesty? They were both going to get hurt if he let this get out of hand.

"I have to go," he said with a glance at his watch, as though he had a crucial appointment somewhere.

"Are you free?" she persisted softly. "Please be frank, Mitch. If there's someone else..."

His head jerked around to look at her. "I work for your father."

Startled, she blinked. "Is that pertinent to you and I?"

"I think it had better be, don't you?"

"Surely you're not telling me we can't be friends because of your job."

Her incredulous expression rocked Mitch. "You don't understand."

"You're right, I don't. I find it hard to believe we're even discussing it." Kim stopped to bite her lip, but she couldn't let him go on thinking that what he did for a living mattered to her. "Mitch, that's a very strange attitude. Do you think Dad would mind?"

"Of course he'd mind, and so should you. Kim, I have to go." Mitch started away. After a few steps he stopped and looked back. She seemed stunned and rooted to the spot. "Coming?"

"Wait a minute." Her voice sounded rather sickly and she hated pressuring him about this, but letting him leave with that ridiculous notion was actually horrifying. "I want to talk about this, Mitch. I have to talk about it. You're badly mistaken about Dad, and..."

"Kim, if you wear me down on this we're both going to be sorry."

Her eyes widened. "Why would you think that?"

His face darkened. "Do you want an affair? That's all it could be."

"My God," she whispered, deeply shaken. "All I've considered for us is..." She took a breath. "No, that's not true. I've had some very adult thoughts about you, Mitch, and I don't ordinarily do that with a man I've just met. Your talking about an affair is..." Her voice broke, and she turned her back to him.

He had hurt her, insulted her, and looking at her slender form he felt like a dog. Stepping closer, he laid a hand on her shoulder. "I'm sorry. It's just that I'm confused about us. Kim, we live in two different worlds. I'm an ordinary guy, a blue-collar worker, and you're..." Words failed him.

She turned to face him. "I'm what, Mitch?" He didn't answer. "You don't know what I am. You don't know who I am. Please believe that I've never come on so strong with another man. I like you, Mitch. I feel you in here." She touched her chest. "And you like me, or you wouldn't be here. Please don't talk about an affair when we haven't even had a date. That hurt, Mitch. You have to know it hurt."

He wanted to crawl under a rock, but Kim wasn't a child and neither was he. She'd plainly confessed to having adult thoughts about him, and his fantasies about her certainly hadn't been a kid's daydreams. This should stop here and now.

But never had he wanted a woman more. Never had just looking at a woman made him as unstable inside as quivering jelly. He'd done no more than briefly touch her shoulder, and he still felt the burn of that innocuous contact.

"What do you want me to do?" he said in a husky whisper.

"Do?" Her eyes darted for a moment. "I'd like to see you again."

"In what capacity?"

Her voice rose. "How can I answer that? It's entirely possible that a few hours in each other's company would completely eradicate any affection we now feel. You're old enough and have to have been around enough to realize..."

He took her arm and put his face practically in hers. "You're asking for trouble, Kim. You know it, I know it. Just don't con yourself on that point, okay?"

She sucked in a sudden breath. "I'm not afraid of trouble, Mitch."

"Maybe you should be."

"Speak for yourself. Until you know me better, don't make judgments for me."

"And in the meantime?"

She had never met anyone like Mitch Conover, and all of his objections had only increased her interest. She dampened her lips. "In the meantime," she said, "I've got two nice steaks in my refrigerator. How about coming to my place for dinner tonight?"

Two

There was a nagging little chant in Mitch's head: *You shouldn't be doing this. You shouldn't be doing this.*

Knowing that it was the lousy damned truth, he still drove from his apartment to Kim's address at seven that night. The affluent area didn't surprise him. The elegant condo complex in a lovely wooded setting didn't surprise him. The only surprise in today's events was that he was ignoring his own common-sense warning to forgo and forget Kim Armstrong.

Mitch located a parking space within the maze of cars and circular streets in the condominium compound, then got out and hiked around to find Kim's building. Her unit was number 104, and he pressed the doorbell with butterflies in his stomach.

The door opened and she stood there with a radiant smile. "Hi."

"Hi."

"Come in." Kim stepped back.

"Thanks." Mitch walked in.

"Did you have any trouble finding the place?" Kim closed the door.

"That's the same question Sarge asked me the evening I went to his house for dinner."

She laughed. "Sorry for the redundancy. It's probably in the genes."

He felt breathless, as though something solid and tight was squeezing his chest. She had changed from her business suit to a long fluffy skirt of cream gauze and a loose overblouse of a coordinated fabric. She was wearing flat-heeled sandals, and he realized that without heels the top of her head only reached his shoulder. Her hair was straight and unadorned; obviously she had shampooed the curl out of it. He liked it this way, and thought of running his fingers through it.

There was a long moment of just looking at each other. Kim drew a breath. "Come to the kitchen. I'm in the middle of making a salad."

He nodded. Kim led him through the living room. He thought her condo was terrific but didn't say so. For that matter, he didn't know what he'd talk about with Kim. Conversation with women had never been a problem, and he didn't like feeling awkward and tongue-tied. But what did they have in common?

"Go ahead and sit at the counter," Kim instructed.

Mitch slid onto a counter stool and watched her reach into the freezer section of the refrigerator. She drew out a frosty bottle of beer. "It's really cold. I saw you with a beer at Dad's, so figured it was your preferred drink. Would you like a glass?"

"The bottle's fine. Thanks." Mitch removed the bottle cap and took a swallow. The icy beer felt good on his parched throat, which shouldn't be parched and was simply because he was with Kim Armstrong. She began working on the salad, ripping crisp lettuce into a large bowl, while standing on the other side of the counter from where he was seated.

She glanced up. "Have you always lived in the Seattle area?"

Obviously she hadn't discussed him with her parents, but why would she? It was possible that she had deliberately omitted him from conversations with the Armstrongs. "I'm from Montana. Born and raised there. I've only lived here for about two years."

"Montana? I love Montana." Kim smiled at him. "I'll bet you grew up on a ranch. I can easily picture you on a horse, Mitch."

He laughed with some wryness. "Sorry, but I had very little to do with horses. I lived in a town, Houghton. My sister married a rancher, though."

"You have a sister? Is she younger or older?"

"Blair's three years younger."

"And you're... how old?"

"Twenty-nine."

Kim smiled. "Although you were too polite to ask, I'm twenty-seven. What about your parents, Mitch? Do they live in Houghton?"

"My parents are dead."

"I'm sorry." Kim began chopping celery on a cutting board. "Then it's just you and your sister. Do you get to see her very often?"

"I haven't seen her since her wedding, but I'm planning on a visit in August." Mitch paused briefly. "I have a vacation coming in August." He waited for her response to that comment, which so effectively pointed out his work status. A new and discomfiting thought flicked through his mind. Until meeting Kim, he'd been proud of his job, proud and satisfied. Was he ashamed to be no more than a working stiff now, one tiny particle within the massive statistics of the lunch-pail brigade? Uneasy with that concept, he picked up his beer for a healthy swallow.

Kim was smiling. "Maybe I'll go with you."

"Pardon?"

"When you go home in August, maybe I'll go with you," she repeated. Stunned, he stared across the counter at her.

She laughed. "Don't look so shocked. I told you I love Montana. Would you hate my traipsing along?"

"You're kidding, aren't you?"

"Smile, Mitch," she said teasingly. "You're much too serious. I bet you never do anything on impulse." Nimbly she began slicing a cucumber. "I'm a little too impulsive sometimes, but..."

"So I've noticed," he interjected.

Her eyes raised to look into his. "I'm still coming on too strong for you, aren't I? That invitation to the opening wasn't an impulse, Mitch. I thought about it for a week before putting your name on the list. I tried telling myself that if you had wanted to see me again, I would have heard from you. But I wouldn't have, would I? You never would have made the first move, would you?"

"No," he said flatly.

"Do you think I'm a predatory female?"

He hesitated, but then the truth came tumbling out. "I think you're the sexiest, most beautiful woman I've ever seen."

Her tongue flicked to dampen her lips. "But you wouldn't have contacted me. Why not?"

"You know why not."

"Because you work for Dad. Mitch, that's so silly. I don't care who you work for."

"You should."

"No, I shouldn't, and neither should you." Kim rinsed her hands at the sink, dried them on a paper towel and put the bowl of salad in the refrigerator. Then she walked around the end of the counter and stood next to Mitch. "You'll never make the second move, either, will you?" she said, her voice low and husky.

His heart started beating like a jackhammer. "Don't, Kim."

She lifted a hand and brushed a lock of hair from his forehead. "I know you like me," she whispered.

He clenched his jaw. "Be careful."

"I don't want to be careful, Mitch. Something hit me very hard the evening we met, and I want to find out what it is."

"If you keep touching me, you will," he warned.

"But don't you like my touching you?" She kept on toying with his hair.

He grabbed her hand. His eyes were dark and glittering. "Maybe you should hear the ground rules."

"What ground rules?" She looked amused.

His thoughts seemed too harsh to recite aloud. *If you want to fool around, fine. But that's as far as it's going with us. Maybe you can ignore who you are, who I am, but I can't.*

"Mitch," she said softly. "What ground rules? What are you thinking?"

"What do you think I'm thinking?" His gruff voice wasn't kind. Her scent and nearness were destroying his will, and he knew how close he was getting to doing something he'd regret.

She twisted her hand in his so that her palm was against his. "Don't be so damned noble," she whispered. "I'm glad we met. I'm glad you're here. So are you or you wouldn't have come at all."

His resistance vanished. Moving quickly he disengaged his hand and lifted it to the back of her neck, where he applied enough pressure to bring down her head. His mouth covered hers in a kiss of utter possession, without gentleness, without tenderness, conveying only the dark swirl of emotions he was feeling.

Its intensity took her breath. Her mind reeled. Mitch affected her like no man ever had. She'd known that from their first meeting, but even her most imaginative fantasies about this man hadn't prepared her for the onslaught of desire she was feeling now. A tremor passed through her body, a shiver that was both delicious and startling.

He didn't prevent her from raising her head and breaking the kiss. She looked into his eyes and saw a challenging "I told you so" glint.

"Maybe I am playing with fire with you," she whispered, and shaped a shaky smile. "And maybe we had better concentrate on those steaks."

With a brooding expression Mitch watched her dart to the other side of the counter. But a little distance and a counter didn't guarantee safety for either of them. That kiss had unleashed a hunger he hadn't known he was capable of feeling. Her response to his lips on hers had indicated the same intense arousal. If he got up right now and went to her, he could probably kiss her into her own bed. The urge to do so was nearly unbearable, especially when Kim's beautiful eyes contained an unmistakable heat that wrung him out.

What he should do was leave right now, before things really got out of hand, and if she came up with any more clever ideas to see each other in the future, he should totally ignore them.

"Tell me about yourself, Mitch," Kim said while taking a plate with the steaks from the refrigerator. The meat was already trimmed and seasoned, Mitch noted.

"What do you want to know?"

Kim arranged the steaks on the broiler pan. "Well, for starters, what do you do in your free time?"

"Mostly attend classes."

Kim raised an eyebrow. "Adult education?"

"Four evenings a week."

"That doesn't leave much time for a private life."

"No, it doesn't." An unusual sensation gripped his vitals. He would like to be able to tell Kim everything there was to tell about himself, about the young boy who'd been devastated by his father's sudden death, about his chaotic feelings of being the man of the family and knowing he couldn't provide for his mother and sister. A hundred stories of growing up in Houghton filled his brain, and another hundred concerning his adulthood, when he'd worked at a dozen different jobs, seeking something from each and never finding it until landing that mechanic's job with Armstrong Paving. He'd like Kim to know that he'd advanced rapidly in the company, and that while his work might not be in the top-ten category of preferred careers, it was important to him.

But confidences and old stories would only bring them another step closer. He would eat her dinner, as it would be rude to do anything else, but that was it. There would be no more meetings, not for any reason.

"I don't have very many free evenings, either," Kim told him. "Many of my clients request evening appointments. Weekends, too." She sent him a smile. "I divide my time between my little studio and visiting clients in their homes. Maybe you'd like to see my studio sometime."

Already their next meeting was in Kim's mind, he realized with his stomach sinking. "Maybe sometime," he allowed, though his tone was noncommittal.

She slid the broiler pan into the oven. "How do you like your steak?"

"Medium rare."

"Me, too. The meat will be done in about eight minutes. I'll put everything else on the table in the dining room."

Mitch let Kim carry the conversational ball during the meal, which appeared easy for her. She chatted about everything from politics to favorite authors and movies to friends of hers that he knew he would never meet. His comments were unemotional and brief, terse, until she told him about a camping trip she'd taken years ago with a group of girls. "Some of our parents drove us to the Olympic peninsula. Have you been there?"

Mitch nodded. "I spent a day there last summer."

Kim smiled impishly. "Did you run into the monster mosquitoes?"

"The what?"

"Every giant mosquito joke you've ever heard couldn't do justice to the reality of the rain forest mosquitoes, Mitch. There were six of us girls and four parents, and all we did for two days and nights was fight the battle of the bugs. After a while it got funny. 'Here they come again,' someone would yell, and we'd all break up."

Mitch couldn't help laughing. 'I didn't meet your monster mosquitoes on the peninsula, but one time a bunch of us drove up to a lake in Canada to do some fishing. Talk about mosquitoes! They were big enough and vicious enough to carry off livestock, which the locals swore they did on a regular basis. We all reeked from mosquito repellent and those buggers still ate us up.''

Kim's laughter, and his own, struck a discordant note in Mitch. Laughing with Kim was almost as dangerous as kissing her. It would be so easy, so great, to just relax and let things happen with them. Not only was she beautiful to look at, she was entertaining and fun to be with. In fact, he couldn't find even one tiny thing about Kim not to like.

But it wasn't a tiny flaw he was looking for, Mitch thought uneasily. A relationship for them was impossible. Even friendship could be perilous, because with so much sexual tension sizzling between them, they wouldn't stay in the friends-only category for long.

Kim suggested having a cup of after-dinner coffee in the living room. Mitch privately decided to drink one cup and get the hell out of there while he still could. Kim escorted him to the living room and then disappeared for a few minutes. When she returned with the coffee, he could tell that she had refreshed her makeup.

She sat down, choosing the chair closest to the sofa, which was where he was sitting. ''I hope you enjoyed dinner. I'm not much of a cook.''

''Dinner was great.''

Thoughtfully she looked at him. ''You know, this would be a good time for you to reciprocate. You could say, 'I'll cook for you next time,' and I would...''

He interrupted. ''No, Kim.'' An array of emotions flickered across her face, delivering him a wallop. Having the power to hurt a person, especially a friendly, warm woman like Kim, was nothing to be proud of. How could he prove to her how thin the ice was under their feet, without hurting her in the process? Then he saw the look of bravado she was giving him.

"Do you really want me to believe we're never going to see each other again?" she questioned. "I don't think you believe it, Mitch. I think you're sitting there trying to reinforce with inane excuses that silly decision to not see me because you're working for Dad. There's absolutely no logic to that decision, and I'd like to debate the subject with you."

"Oh, you would?"

"Yes. Are you willing?"

He sat back. "You go first."

"Fine." Kim took a deep breath. "First of all, neither of my parents are even slightly inclined toward prejudice of any kind. Secondly, if Dad didn't think you were doing a good job, you wouldn't be working for him. That alone proves to me that he holds you in high regard. Thirdly, I've supported myself for five years now, and my parents are proud of my independence. I know they would never interfere in my private life."

Mitch's expression was calm. "You've missed the point completely."

"I have?"

"You never mentioned how I might feel about the whole thing."

"Which is?"

His deceptive casualness vanished, and he leaned forward, conveying his tension. "I won't get ahead in the company by kissing up to the boss's daughter."

Kim stared for the longest time. His expression was grim, completely serious. He actually believed in the validity of what he'd just said, and to her it was the most ridiculous, groundless hogwash she'd ever heard.

It was also insulting. Kim's chin came up. "The Armstrongs are neither small-minded nor naive. Any of us could spot a fortune hunter a mile off. Believe me, you don't fit the description."

"And I don't intend to try." Mitch got to his feet. "I think it's time I left. Thanks for dinner."

The burst of anger she felt surprised Kim, but it drove her to her feet. "We could have something very good together!"

Mitch scowled. "Do you want me to show you what we could have? The only thing we could have?"

Kim backed up a step. Without question her remark had ruffled Mitch's emotions, and the dark expression on his face was daunting. But her own emotions weren't exactly placid at the moment, and she wasn't wrong about this, dammit, he was!

"I doubt that you could prove anything to me on the spur-of-the-moment," she said with some sarcasm. "Relationships take time. Your refusal to—" He reached for her, and the words died in her throat. "What're you doing?"

The question was a waste of breath and effort when what he was doing was so obvious. She was in his arms, clamped to his chest, stunned by his heat and hard strength.

"This is what we could have," he mumbled thickly before settling his lips on hers.

Skyrockets went off in Kim's head. Her knees were suddenly weak and trembling. The energy of Mitch's kiss was thrilling, and the physical pleasure the greatest of her life. She moaned deep in her throat and leaned into him, clasping her arms around his waist. The only thing he was proving to her was what she'd known all along: they were terrific together!

She felt his tongue in her mouth and his hands on her back and hips, and not an objection to anything he was doing could be found anywhere in her system. Rather, she snuggled closer.

Groaning, Mitch raised his head and looked at her flushed face and glazed eyes. He tried to speak gruffly. "Is this what you want?"

Her tongue flicked to her own lips and his taste sent her senses flying. "Only an idiot would say no," she whispered huskily. "But it's only one portion of what we could have."

His eyes flashed. "The other portion is best handled in the bedroom. I'm ready if you are."

Indeed he was ready. She could feel just how ready in the pressure of his arousal against her lower abdomen. She was ready, too. Her heart was beating crazily, and the bittersweet sting of desire held her in a viselike grip.

But . . . it was too soon for the bedroom. A few kisses, no matter how tantalizing, how sweetly tempting, did not constitute a relationship. There was something about Mitch that smacked of permanency to Kim. She'd felt it from their first meeting. Easily she could see him in her future. For that matter, visualizing the future without him caused a painful backlash of emotion she had no desire to face.

Her eyes searched his. "You're asking me to believe that sex is all we could ever have together. I don't believe it, Mitch. I won't believe it."

He blinked. His arms were still holding her. Her warmth still penetrated his clothing and skin. What had he proven, other than the fact of their mutual attraction? What had he been trying to prove? That he wouldn't marry the boss's daughter come hell or high water? He couldn't say that aloud, not when they'd spent maybe three hours together. She would think him demented if he verbally retreated from the idea of marriage when they barely knew each other.

But if marriage was out, what was left? With this kind of explosive passion between them, they sure as hell couldn't be only friends!

"I'll make love to you right now if that's what you want," he said hoarsely. "But then that's the end of it. No repeats, no more meetings, no calls, no—"

"Just stop it!" Immediately Kim's voice softened, and she brought a hand up to touch his face. "Mitch, I will not give your stubborn, prideful attitude any credence. You need to get to know Dad and Mother better, and you need to know me better. The Armstrongs . . ."

Brusquely he broke away from her, stepping back. "You're not listening to me. Are you so accustomed to getting your own way that you ride roughshod over anyone else's opinion?"

Kim gasped. "That's a cheap shot! You seem to enjoy saying mean things to me. Is that what *you're* accustomed to?"

They fell silent and looked at each other, their differing viewpoints weighting the path of their gazes.

"We don't think alike," Mitch finally muttered. "But why would we? I'm going to go." He turned and walked toward the living room doorway.

Kim hesitated, then followed. At the last moment, she darted around Mitch and leaned her back against the condo's front door. "I don't think we're so different," she said to Mitch's dark and glowering face.

"Let it alone, okay?"

Embarrassment suddenly infused Kim. Never before had she chased a man or begged for his attention, and her behavior today could hardly be categorized as anything else. But he was so damned stubborn, and so maddening. His attitude was brand-new to her. Dating the boss's daughter seemed like a deadly sin to him, which was so utterly ludicrous she could barely grasp the concept.

And, yet, he'd kissed her like a hungry man. It hurt that he liked her and couldn't admit it. *Wouldn't* admit it.

Embarrassed or not, this wasn't over. She put her heart in a smile and spoke softly. "We will meet again, Mitch."

"Don't count on it. Let me leave, Kim."

"If I said yes to an affair would you be so anxious to leave?"

"A very brief affair," he reminded.

"Oh, I'm not so sure of that. Usually one potato chip leads to..."

"Dammit, we're not talking about potato chips!" Mitch's face was flushed. Their kisses were still on his lips. He could still feel her in his arms, and though his opinion about the two of them being irrevocably mismatched was genuine, arguing with a beautiful woman over an affair, brief or otherwise, had a somewhat farcical quality. "Stand out of the way so I can leave," he demanded.

"I won't be bullied, Mitch," she said softly, but Kim's inner arguments were losing strength. Obviously nothing she said was going to change his stiff-necked male mind. "Someday you're going to regret this," she added while stepping away from the door.

"I already regret it," Mitch growled. He grabbed the knob and opened the door. "Goodbye, Kim."

"It's not goodbye for me, so I think I'll just say so long for now."

He could hear the tears in her voice, and for a moment he stopped and closed his eyes against a rush of empathy. But empathy was another dangerous emotion, and he squared his shoulders and stepped out into the night.

He drove home, alternately cursing his own stupidity in going to Kim's in the first place and her determination. Yes, something could happen between them if she wasn't an Armstrong, or he didn't work for Sarge. But facts were facts, and he'd be a damned fool to get involved when he knew better. The mere thought of wooing the boss's daughter gave him cold chills, let alone the outcome to such a relationship, should it endure.

"No, thanks," he mouthed with bitterness, when ordinarily he wasn't a bitter man. Life had never been particularly easy for the Conovers, but certainly during the last few years things had started looking up. His sister was happily married in Montana and he had a good job in Seattle. What was more, he'd managed to save some money and start building a real future for himself. Fooling around with Kim Armstrong could set him back forty paces. "No, thanks," he repeated aloud. He shouldn't have kissed her, but as he had, his most sensible course now as to avoid repeating the mistake.

If she maneuvered him into another meeting, he'd do his best to remember today.

Hopefully, there would be no more meetings.

Three

___

Kim took a handful of generously cut fabric swatches from her service bag and spread them out on the coffee table. "These are the fabrics I mentioned on the phone, Mrs. Hildebrand. Any of them would coordinate dramatically with your bedroom carpet." While Mrs. Hildebrand studied the swatches, Kim talked about textures and colors. The woman had requested a complete redecoration of her bedroom suite—other than carpeting—and the swatches were samples of drapery and upholstery fabrics, suggestions, really, as Kim left final decisions up to her clients.

"They're unique and lovely, Kim, but aren't they a little lightweight?" Mrs. Hildebrand gently fingered the fabrics.

"Lightweight but durable, Mrs. Hildebrand. They will make up beautifully," Kim replied. "And they have a natural tendency to drape and flow." Every client's needs were different. Mrs. Hildebrand, though obviously well-to-do, was a practical woman and durability had been high on her list of priorities.

The conversation went on for nearly an hour. Mrs. Hildebrand was still undecided when Kim got up to go. "I'll leave the swatches with you, Mrs. Hildebrand. Take your time. Call me when you're ready for the next step. If, in the end, none of these fabrics are perfect for what you have in mind, let me know and I'll work up another plan."

The woman thanked Kim and saw her to the door. Kim deposited her service bag and purse on the front seat of her four-wheel-drive vehicle and got in. Sighing, she started the engine and drove away from the elegant Hildebrand home.

As was happening in nearly every free moment, Mitch Conover's image took shape in her mind. Driving through the residential area to reach a main thoroughfare, Kim chewed on her bottom lip and thought about Mitch. If she had ever felt the same unusual emotions with another man, Mitch might not be so important. But she hadn't, and he was. How could she get through to him? How could she even see him again when he was so determined to elude another meeting?

The situation was ludicrous. Mitch's attitude was ludicrous. As for her, she felt adolescent and awkward, a little humiliated that she would even consider chasing a man who so obviously didn't want to be caught.

And, yet, she had sensed some extremely potent feelings in Mitch that day at her condo. After ten days she could still feel the intensity of his kisses, and if he was so positive about their relationship being a mistake, why had he kissed her at all?

Sighing again, Kim slowed down to comply with the signs denoting some road construction ahead. Traffic came to a crawl, and she inched along for two blocks before seeing the actual construction site. Then she smiled. It was one of her father's projects. The trucks and equipment all bore the company name, Armstrong Paving and Asphalt.

The project fronted a huge shopping complex, and the heavy traffic was limited to two lanes and moving at a snail's pace. Kim checked her watch. She had an appointment at the studio in thirty minutes and hated keeping a client waiting, but there was no quick way around this congestion.

Unless...? Spotting a turn into the shopping complex, Kim cranked the wheel to the right and drove into the mall's parking lot. By cutting across it and driving a few back streets, she could take another route to her studio.

Beginning to maneuver through the parked cars, she suddenly slammed on the brakes. Not thirty feet away was Mitch! Kim stared, hardly believing her own eyes. He was talking to two men, co-workers, obviously, and Lord, he was handsome. Just looking at him set Kim's heart to pounding. Why did he affect her like this? Why did the mere sight of him make her stomach draw up into a tight knot?

Her lips thinned in determination. She couldn't let this opportunity pass. Looking around, she realized that neither could she sit there and block traffic. But she didn't have time to locate a parking spot. Mitch wasn't going to stand there indefinitely, she realized frantically as the two men began walking away from him. She had to do something fast.

She leaned on the horn. Apparently accustomed to traffic noises, Mitch never even glanced in her direction. Pressing lightly on the gas, she drove closer and stopped again. Rolling down the window, she called, "Mitch!" He turned with a frown, which intensified when he saw her. His forbidding expression was daunting, but Kim gathered her courage and called, "Hi! Got a minute?"

Mitch ambled over to her vehicle and leaned down to peer in the window. "This is a surprise."

She smiled. "Yes, isn't it? I was planning to cut through the parking lot to avoid the traffic snarl and there you were. I couldn't resist saying hello." Her gaze flicked down to the open neck of his shirt. Even the sight of his bare throat gave her goose bumps. "How've you been?"

"Can't complain." Why did she have to be so damned pretty? Inwardly Mitch groaned. No woman should have Kim Armstrong's lustrous, luscious hair, nor possess eyes that color. He'd been moderately successful at forgetting her, and he didn't need this reminder.

Kim searched for a topic. "Looks like you've got quite a project going here."

"It's small. Just some patchwork. We'll be out of here by tomorrow night."

"And then?"

"My crew is scheduled for three miles of paving near Olympia."

"Your crew? Are you a supervisor?"

"Yes."

"How long will you be in Olympia?"

"About ten days, two weeks. Depends."

"Are you out of town very much, Mitch?"

"Off and on. You must know how the company functions." Mitch straightened up. "There's a car behind you."

"Oh, I guess I have to move. Mitch, I'd like to talk to you." She was speaking too rapidly, but the driver behind her was getting impatient. On edge, she cast her eyes around for a parking space and spotted one. "I'm going to park over there. Can you take a few minutes and talk to me?"

"Kim..."

His reluctance seemed to shred her insides. Something had to be seriously wrong with her when she had to forcibly beat back the urge to beg.

"Another time then," she said with forced brightness. "See you, Mitch."

"Yeah, see you."

Driving away, Kim realized she was trembling. Five minutes in Mitch's presence had reduced her to a quivering bowl of jelly. Angrily she slapped the steering wheel. This had to stop. She had never begged a man in her life and she had just come very close to doing so.

Mitch got back to work when Kim drove away, but he was able to control his physical movements much more effectively than he could his thoughts. He hated hurting Kim and every meeting they had ended up that way, all because she refused to accept his position regarding the two of them.

Mitch shuddered at the thought of Sarge finding out that his daughter was dating one of his employees. One of two things was bound to happen. Either Sarge would despise him for it and possibly find a reason to let him go, or Sarge *wouldn't* despise him for it and would possibly start showing favoritism. Neither option appealed to Mitch, and getting down to brass tacks, the second was the worst. If he made even one small step in the company because of favoritism, he would quit his job without a heartbeat's hesitation.

But that was what Kim didn't grasp. Maybe she couldn't. Maybe her life had been so indulged she wasn't capable of understanding how important it was for a man to attain his own success.

What was so aggravating was that no matter how sensible his stand, Mitch couldn't deny the enormous attraction he felt for Kim Armstrong. Seeing her so unexpectedly had upset his equilibrium, and his concentration. By the conclusion of the workday he wasn't positive which end was up, and he drove to his apartment with a taut, uneasy expression on his face.

The silence of the apartment seemed unusually heavy. He had a class this evening and his normal routine included a shower, some supper and an hour of study before leaving for Seattle University. The shower was mandatory and accomplished quickly, though absentmindedly. Dressed in clean clothes and in the kitchen a few minutes later, Mitch stared blankly into the refrigerator and decided nothing it contained looked good, and that he would stop at a fast-food outlet on his way to the university.

He went to his desk in the living room, sat down and opened a book. But the text swam before his eyes and he slammed the book shut within minutes. Rising restlessly, he eyed the telephone. The urge to speak to Kim, to apologize for his rudeness, seemed all-important. She was, getting down to basics, Sarge's daughter, and rudeness to her was almost as bad as it would be to Sarge.

The Seattle telephone directory was huge and cumbersome. Mitch brought it to the desk and opened it to the *A* listings. His heart sank at the dozens of Armstrongs. On closer examination, however, there were only four that he thought could be Kim's number.

His third call got results. Kim answered. "Hello?"

Relieved, though immediately on edge, Mitch cleared his throat. "Hi. This is Mitch."

Still smarting from the rebuff Mitch had administered earlier in the day, Kim broke a lengthy silence with, "Mitch who?"

"How many Mitches do you know?"

"Well, let me see. There's Mitch Stafford . . . and Mitch Capelli . . . and . . ."

"Mitch Conover," he said brusquely, wondering if she weren't manufacturing names to annoy him. Obviously she was ticked, and he couldn't blame her. Wouldn't he be irritated if someone had brushed him off the way he'd done to her? "I called to apologize," he said quietly. "I wasn't very nice today and I'm sorry."

Kim's breath caught. An apology was the last thing she'd expected. "That's decent of you," she murmured. "Thanks."

"You're welcome."

Wondering if this call had a second chapter, Kim sat down. Mitch had gotten right to his apology and could be planning to make this conversation very short. His next comment—possibly no more than a goodbye—should tell the tale. She waited.

"By the way, I noticed your four-wheeler today. Nice unit," Mitch said.

The hint of a satisfied smile tipped Kim's lips. His introducing an unnecessary topic was proof of his interest, however much he kept dodging the truth.

"I like it," Kim said calmly. "It's great in bad weather."

"I imagine so. Surprised me, though. Not that I've actually wondered what you drove, but if I had, I wouldn't have come up with a four-wheeler."

"Oh? Why is that, Mitch?"

He hesitated. Telling her that she fit some pretty little sports car much better than a sturdy, sensible vehicle could be a leading remark. For that matter, he had made his apology and should tell her goodbye.

But a sudden surge of rebellion stopped him. Since moving to Seattle, he hadn't met one other woman who'd affected him like Kim did. Before that, in Montana, his female friends had never advanced beyond the fun-for-a-day-or-a-night category. What made Kim so special escaped him. She was pretty, even beautiful, but he'd known and did know other pretty women. In a flash of enlightenment he realized that he and Kim connected in a mysteriously sensual way. Even on the phone he felt it. His skin was tingling from hearing her faint breathing, of all things.

"Kim..."

"Yes?" It was almost a whisper, husky in Mitch's ear.

"Today you said something about talking. Would you like to..." He paused briefly and drew a breath "...to meet?"

A dizzying joy rocketed through Kim. She sat up straighter. Her eyes became brighter. "Yes, I would. When?"

"I can't tonight. I've got to leave for my class in a few minutes. But sometime this weekend would be all right."

He sounded strained, as though disliking what he was doing. And, yet, she hadn't wrangled him into suggesting a meeting. It was all his doing and it was lifting Kim to the stars. "When are you going to Olympia?"

"We'll start hauling down the equipment on Monday."

"Shall we plan something for Saturday then?" she said softly.

"Saturday would be fine."

Kim interjected a lighter, almost teasing note. "I could take you for a ride in my four-wheeler."

Mitch took a moment to digest the idea, deciding that it might do Kim good to see how he lived. "Why don't you pick me up." He recited his address.

"I have an appointment on Saturday morning. Shall we make it around two?" she asked, realizing how breathless her voice sounded. But Mitch's change of heart was astounding, elating, and she could barely control her speaking tone.

"Two is fine. See you then."

"Thank you for calling, Mitch. See you on Saturday." After hanging up, Kim sat there smiling, nearly bursting with excitement. Analyzing that call wasn't possible. Something had altered Mitch's attitude, and she didn't know him well enough to figure out what it was.

But maybe it didn't matter. Maybe nothing did. Not only had he called and apologized, he had actually asked for a date!

Whooping happily, Kim got up and danced around the room.

In Mitch's apartment, he wasn't quite so exhilarated. In fact, he was wondering if he hadn't lost his mind. Cussing under his breath, he set himself to gathering his books to leave for the university.

Regardless, during the drive and while grabbing a burger at a fast-food restaurant, he couldn't think of anything other than seeing Kim on Saturday.

It wasn't at all comforting to realize that he was caught in the grip of something bigger than common sense, and he went to his class in an unusually somber mood.

On Friday evening Kim had dinner with her parents at their home. Several times Mitch's name was on the tip of her tongue, but each time she bit it back. Sarge and Sara hadn't attempted to choose her friends since high school, and even then they had trusted her own intelligence and given her every leeway. They were great parents and always had been. Looking at them around the table, Kim knew they would be shocked to hear that Mitch Conover thought they might be prejudiced against him merely because he was an employee. It was information that could backfire and cause them to look askance at Mitch. It was information better left unsaid.

Besides, Mitch must have come to his senses on that subject. They liked each other, they were going to see each other, and who her parents were had no bearing on the relationship.

"You seem unusually up tonight," Sara commented to her daughter. "Things must be going well for you."

Kim's smile was a yard wide. "Things are going very well, Mother."

It was a normal family meal, with good food, good conversation and the warmth of genuine affection.

Kim left with a kiss and hug from both parents. But the song in her heart wasn't caused by the congeniality of a pleasant evening with the two people she loved most in the world. Mitch was causing that, and because she would see him tomorrow.

Tomorrow....

Life was wonderful.

The Seattle area had been enjoying clear skies for over a week, but Saturday arrived with murky gray clouds and a misty rainfall, disappointing Kim as she had been visualizing a carefree afternoon with Mitch in the sunshine. They could still take a ride, of course. If the inhabitants of the Pacific coast let a little rain keep them inside, they would end up living like moles.

But the damp weather made her dress differently than she would have had it been sunny. Instead of a skirt she put on jeans, and in place of the pretty peasant blouse she preferred, she settled for a blue-and-white T-shirt with sleeves. It wasn't cold outside but neither was it warm, and leaving for her morning appointment, Kim tossed a lightweight jacket into the back seat of her four-wheeler.

The appointment went well. Kim nailed down another decorating job—a large, older home in the Palisades section of the city—then spent the next two hours in her studio going over the sketches she had made of the house. She had also taken notes of the owner's preferences in style and color, and as usual when starting a new project, her creative juices were flowing.

But, as had occurred last night with her folks, the excitement in her system was mostly because of seeing Mitch again. She was, Kim realized, almost giddy over their afternoon date. Never before had she known a man who could fill her with such anticipation over a simple drive together. It had to mean something. Kim paused with her notes and sketches to give that idea consideration. Her career had kept her so busy for so long, she hadn't missed not having a serious one-on-one relationship with a man. Going back seven or eight years, there had been an important guy for a while. Now she had trouble recalling his face, so she understood how a woman could believe she was in love and then have the whole thing fizzle out.

Still, a comparison of that relationship to what was happening with her and Mitch didn't quite line up. She felt differently about Mitch than about anyone else she'd ever known, but what, precisely, made those feelings different? Was she physically smitten by his dark and brooding good looks? By his kisses? Surely she was above falling for a man merely because he activated her libido.

Yet she couldn't deny that the excitement gripping her was sexually charged. Nor should she try to deny anything, Kim thought with sudden fervor. She was, after all, an adult and the mistress of her own fate.

But, thinking sensibly, perhaps she should attempt caution on one thing, and that was to guard against falling harder for Mitch than he did for her. Frowning reflectively, Kim went back in time to a college girlfriend who had nearly ruined her own life by falling for a man who hadn't returned her affection. The girl had drawn all of her friends, particularly Kim, into the scenario, and everyone concerned had ended up unhappy and ultimately at odds with each other.

With that memory vivid in her mind, Kim vowed that she would involve no one else in her and Mitch's relationship, especially not her parents. Deep down she had high hopes for the two of them—something else she couldn't deny—but until she and Mitch knew each other much better than they did, neither friends nor family needed to hear that they were dating.

Kim smiled. Dating. She liked that word when applied to Mitch.

At 1:00 p.m. she put away her sketches and notes and went to the small bathroom in her studio to brush her hair and refresh her lipstick. Her eyes positively glowed in the mirror, and there was a flush to her cheeks that hadn't been there before Mitch's call. There was every possibility, she thought in a moment of utter fantasy, of her exiting her car at Mitch's address and walking to his front door without her feet even touching the ground.

Laughing at the idea of walking on air, Kim grabbed her purse, locked the studio and headed into the rain for the parking lot and her four-wheeler.

She arrived at Mitch's address at ten minutes to two and saw a sprawling apartment complex. Driving through the parking lot, she located his building and parked as close to it as she could. Bounding through the rain, she climbed a flight of stairs to the building's second story and pushed Mitch's doorbell.

The door opened and there he was. "Hi."

"Hi." She couldn't seem to stop smiling, or to breathe normally. If short breaths, a pounding heart and an incessant urge to grin were any measure, she had it bad for Mr. Conover.

He stepped back. "Come in."

"Thanks."

While Kim's gaze moved around his tiny living room, Mitch fought a desire to kiss her. Kissing those delectable lips had been his first thought upon seeing her. Holding her. Touching her. He sucked in an unsteady breath.

"Darling apartment," Kim remarked. She sent Mitch a teasing smile. "Typically male."

If he wanted to be deadly serious right now, he could take umbrage at her choice of adjectives. His apartment was not "darling." It was small and plain and a place to sleep, study, change clothes and occasionally throw together a meal.

But there was a giddiness in his body that crowded out "serious." He cocked an eyebrow. "Oh? I didn't know apartments had gender."

"Most definitely." Kim stepped to the sofa. "Leather furniture. Unadorned walls. Masculine colors. Oh, yes, definitely male."

Amused, Mitch folded his arms across his chest and leaned against a wall. "And just what makes a color masculine or feminine?"

Kim laughed lightly. "Do you see any pinks in here? Any lavenders? Pink for girls, blue for boys. Everything in here is blue."

"Don't try to convince me you follow that old rule in your work, Kimberly Armstrong. Remember that I saw those models you decorated."

"But I'm a professional, Mitch Conover," she teased back. "And those models were decorated strictly for eye appeal. For impact. One's home should reflect..." She stopped and grinned. "A lesson on home decor would bore you to tears. How many rooms do you have?"

Mitch pushed away from the wall. "Three rooms and a bath. The kitchen's through that door, and the bedroom's over there."

"Mind if I peek?"

"Help yourself." Mitch watched her dart to the kitchen doorway and peer in, then open the door to the bedroom.

"It's small but efficiently arranged," Kim commented, turning to face him. "Similar to my condo."

Mitch smirked. "Hardly."

Kim's eyes widened slightly. "But it is, Mitch. My kitchen is a little larger and I have a second bedroom, but my living room is no bigger, and..." She glanced to the dining area of the room "...my eating area is about the same size."

"Your condo is terrific," Mitch retorted. "And this apartment is nothing more than a place to hang my hat."

"It's not decorated! I spent weeks decorating the condo. Well, not weeks, but I put in many evenings and several weekends on wallpapering and painting."

Mitch was losing interest in the topic. For one thing, neither Kim nor anyone else would ever convince him that a little wallpaper and paint would make this drab apartment into something special, as her condo was. The other distraction in his mind was the sight of this lady in jeans. They were old jeans, faded and soft, and they hugged her legs and hips in a most beguiling manner. He knew she shouldn't be here. He knew he shouldn't be looking at her with profound admiration and that hot, bittersweet ache of desire. And, yet, the crazy joy in his soul wouldn't permit him to ruin the day with another spate of honesty.

"Should we go?" he asked, worried that hanging around here together might destroy his diminishing grasp on reality. A drive was safe. One of them, at least, would be occupied with the road and traffic.

"I'm ready when you are," Kim replied. "You might want to take a jacket. The rain isn't a downpour, but it's steady."

Nodding, Mitch left the room. Instead of a jacket, he put on a tan suede vest, and in a moment of obstinacy—Kim should see that he was just an old country boy at heart—he slapped his favorite cowboy hat on his head.

Her smile flashed as big as all outdoors when he came out of the bedroom. "You look great in that hat! I love it!"

Her enthusiasm hit Mitch as hard as a blow to the belly would have. Kim was a sweetheart, a doll, the kind of woman for whom any guy would happily stand on his head in the middle of the freeway, if he thought it would gain her interest. And she liked him. Her smiles were for him, because of him.

It was sobering knowledge. Perversely, it was also *exciting* knowledge. He shaped a grin. "Come on, princess, let's go."

"Princess? Hey, I like that." She did like it. She liked it so much she smiled all the way to her four-wheeler. Even the rain felt wonderful. Nothing was going to mar this day, nothing!

"You drive," she said before they got in.

"Sure, if you want." Mitch opened the passenger door for her to scoot in, then bounded around the front of the vehicle to climb behind the wheel. He looked at her. "Where to?"

Kim shrugged. "There are dozens of places to go. Do you have any preference? What haven't you seen of the area?"

"I've looked around quite a lot. Have you got a favorite spot?"

"Um...not really. I love the islands. Would you like to take a ferry ride?"

"In the rain?"

Kim grinned and held out the key. "Sure, why not? A little rain won't hurt us."

Mitch inserted the key in the ignition and started the motor. "A ferry ride it is. You play navigator and tell me which way to go."

"Be careful of my directions. They might take you into dangerous territory," she teased in a softly sensual voice.

His eyes stayed on her. "I think I stumbled into dangerous territory the night we met, princess."

Kim's breath caught. "Maybe we both did," she said huskily.

Mitch hesitated, then nodded. "I guess we did. Fasten your seat belt, princess. It's takeoff time."

Four

———

"It's raining much harder." Kim made the observation while Mitch was driving onto the ferry.

He braked to a stop and turned off the engine. Vehicles were in front of them, behind them and on either side, and no one was getting out of his car to brave the rain. Most of the ferries within the Puget Sound transportation system were closed conveyances. This was one of the smaller units and open, and the rain was pelting Kim's four-wheeler, seemingly with a vengeance.

But the interior of the vehicle was warm and cozy. Mitch cracked his window about an inch and turned in the seat to view his companion. "Guess we could have picked a better day for a ferry ride."

Kim was perfectly content. The rain made a pleasant sound and Mitch was with her. But to be agreeable, she murmured, "Guess we could have." After a moment, she added, "This is nice, though." She knew Mitch was looking at her, and she brought her head around to see him. Their eyes met and held, and it was as though they were suddenly miles from anyone else instead of in the midst of dozens of cars and probably a hundred people. There was a glimmer of understanding in their gazes, and turmoil, so much turmoil. Even the air around them seemed turbulent.

Mitch looked away first. His pulse was speeding and all he could think of was making love with Kim. His mind was dizzy from erotic images and his tongue felt too thick to speak.

Clangs and bangs outside announced the closing of the ferry ramp. Engines rumbled to life. The ship began moving. The internal pressure building in Kim made her restive, and she wished the sun were shining and they could get out. An urge to slide across the seat and see how Mitch would react was barely controllable. He could look at her with the most yearning expression, but would he ever do anything about it? Dare she bring it out in the open and ask him why not? Would it be too bold, too pushy, of her to force another discussion about attitudes? Dammit, was he still hung up on her being his boss's daughter?

Striving to calm herself, Kim drew a long breath. Her voice was even, more toneless than anything. "Have you taken any of the ferries before?"

"I took the one to Victoria last summer." Mitch, too, sounded emotionless. Kim stiffened. They were both holding back, pretending they hadn't noticed the tension of that exchanged look. "The sun was out that day. I enjoyed the trip."

"Yes, it's a very pleasant...trip." What an insipid conversation, Kim thought. Would the whole afternoon pass with the two of them acting like strangers? She had started out so enthused, so lighthearted, and she wanted more from today than dull, noncommittal conversation.

She sent him a quick glance and saw the jutting stubbornness of his jaw. Determination exploded within her. She would make him laugh again if it killed her, and somehow, some way, she would also make him forget that her name was Armstrong!

"Let me try on your hat," she said in a much warmer voice. Mitch's head jerked around. Kim smiled. "Don't look so surprised. Share your hat, cowboy. I've been thinking about buying one, and I'd like to check out the effect first."

An indulgent grin formed on Mitch's lips. He took off the hat and held it out. "It'll be too big, but have a look at it."

"Thanks." Kim took the hat and flipped down the visor above the windshield to expose the mirror on its underside. She set the big hat on her head at a cocky angle and looked at her reflection. "Not bad. What do you think?"

"Other than being three sizes too big, it looks pretty good," Mitch drawled. "Here, wear it like this." Reaching out, he adjusted the hat to sit lower on her forehead. His grin flashed. "Now you look like a cowgirl."

But the hat had slipped lower and all but covered Kim's eyes. "More like a cow," she retorted.

Mitch chuckled. "Princess, you couldn't look like a cow if you tried."

His laugh thrilled Kim. Smiling, she removed the hat and handed it back. "It looks better on you." Mitch tossed the hat into the back seat. "I also like that vest," Kim said. "It's very...masculine." She had almost said sexy, which was more accurate. That suede vest made his shoulders look ten feet wide, and also gave her goose bumps thinking about how it would feel to snuggle against it.

"So I have a masculine apartment and a masculine vest," Mitch said with another chuckle.

"Everything about you is masculine, my dear," Kim said with a suggestive waggle of her eyebrows. "You make me think of— No, I'd better not say that. You'd get that uptight expression in your eyes again. Do you know that your eyes are almost the same color as mine?"

"No way," Mitch scoffed. "Your eyes are violet. Mine are blue."

"Your eyes are as violet as mine," she insisted.

"They are not."

"Take a look." Kim pointed at the mirror on the visor, hoping he wouldn't think to check his own visor, which also had a mirror. It worked. Mitch slid over and peered into her mirror. His thigh pressed into hers, and their heads came together as they both used the same small mirror. "See?" she said with sudden breathlessness. "Very close to the same color."

"Well, I'll be damned," Mitch mumbled, stunned that she was right. He turned his head slightly and seemed surprised to find her face a breath away from his, her lips nearly touching his. "Kim..." He sounded like a rusty hinge, he realized dimly, hoarse, out of breath.

"Mitch," she whispered, and lifted her chin a fraction to put her lips practically under his. It was a blatant appeal for a kiss, she knew it, he knew it, and they began a stare down that all but sizzled.

"Damn, you're something," Mitch whispered raggedly. His eyes probed hers. "You know what's going to happen if we don't keep this under control, don't you?"

She wove her fingers into his hair. "Yes, I know."

"And you don't care?"

Her tongue flicked to moisten her lips. "I care so much I don't know what hit me. Kiss me, Mitch," she whispered.

He closed his eyes and let their mouths unite. At once his blood began roaring and racing. Her lips were sweet and soft and with a heavenly flavor. Her scent filled his nostrils and then his brain. His hands formed fists, and he deliberately, through great effort, kept them away from her.

But Kim had no such prohibitive inclinations, and she brought a hand to his chest to explore that marvelously sexy vest. Her tongue glided over his lips and sought entrance, and she didn't even attempt to stifle the low moan deep in her throat. Yet he only parted his lips a little, withholding the intimacy of his mouth from her.

She managed to speak, to whisper, "Kiss me the way you want to."

He jerked his head up. His eyes were dark and smoldering. "If I did what I wanted . . . !" He flung himself back across the seat to the driver's side.

The trembling in Kim's body made even her voice quake. "You will do what you want eventually."

"Don't count on it." In an angry motion, Mitch wiped the moisture from his mouth.

His wiping away her kiss made Kim see red. She battled her temper and a spate of harsh words, while fussing with her hair in the visor mirror to cover her ruffled emotions. But it was such an inane reason to fight. Mitch not only had the power to thrill her, he was able to hurt her, and she was getting in entirely too deep with a man who kept backing off.

She managed to put aside the anger, and the fear, which was brand-new and startling, and to speak almost normally. "The ferry engines are shutting down. We must be approaching the island."

Her abrupt change of mood surprised Mitch, but if she could forget what had just happened, so could he. Well, maybe not forget, but the day would be ruined if he didn't make an effort.

"Sounds like it," he agreed.

In minutes the ferry had docked and the vehicles began driving off of it. Mitch started the four-wheeler and followed the flow of traffic. He cast Kim a glance. "How about something to eat?"

"Great," she replied, putting a lilt in her voice she certainly didn't feel.

The afternoon went surprisingly well. Both Kim and Mitch recovered from their encounter on the ferry and enjoyed the drive around the small island. When the sun peeked through the clouds around four, they got out and hiked a stretch of rocky beach. Later, in one of the little towns where they had stopped for a soft drink, Mitch said, "Wait here for a minute, okay?"

"What for?"

"I see something in that shop. Wait here."

Kim shrugged. "Sure."

Mitch came out ten minutes later with a package, which he promptly handed over. "It's for you."

"For me?" Mystified, Kim opened the sack and peered in. "What in the world . . . ?" She pulled out a soft, cream-colored suede vest. "Mitch, it's gorgeous."

"And it's *not* masculine."

Kim laughed in delight. "Definitely not masculine. Mitch, this had to be expensive."

"The cost doesn't matter. I wanted you to have it. Try it on."

Slipping on the vest, Kim felt a crazy surge of tears in her eyes. She should refuse such an expensive gift, and knew if she did he would be hurt. For some reason she couldn't hurt him, not knowingly, but why should she feel so cautious about inflicting pain when he was not? He had to know that his constant rebuffs drove spikes into her heart. If he didn't, he was a lot denser than she'd thought.

Kim snuggled the vest around herself. Mitch wasn't at all dense. Whatever was going on between them, he felt everything she did, every thrill, every hurt, every nuance of voice and gesture.

"Thank you," she said huskily. "I love it."

"It suits you."

"Yes, I think it does." *But why do you retreat as you do and then buy me a costly gift like this?*

Mitch glanced at the sky. The brief spurt of sunshine had vanished in a pall of heavy clouds. "Maybe we should head back. Do you know what time the next ferry leaves?"

Kim checked her watch. "In a half hour."

They returned to the four-wheeler and drove to the ferry landing. Kim cherished her new vest and kept stroking its fine, soft leather. Other than her parents, no one had ever given her such a meaningful gift. What should she think of a man who would, on impulse, walk into a shop and buy an expensive gift for a woman he tried so hard to keep at arm's length?

The disturbing question made Kim sigh. They were waiting in line to board the ferry, and Mitch sent her a glance. "Are you okay?"

"I'm…" Kim hesitated then decided she had little to lose by being honest. "I'm questioning you and I, Mitch."

"Which I've been doing since we met," he said in a dark, somber tone.

"Not in the same way."

"A debatable remark."

"Then debate it, dammit!"

Mitch's eyes widened. "You're angry."

"I'm mystified. I'm a little numb, a lot excited and yes, partly angry. And you want to know why? It's because of you."

"I already knew that," Mitch muttered. "Kim, I don't want to fight with you."

"No, but you want to do *something* with me, and it's driving you crazy." Kim stared at him. "Isn't it?"

"Damned right it's driving me crazy. *You're* driving me crazy." Groaning, he put his head down on the steering wheel. "Why'd you have to be Sarge's daughter?"

Every ounce of passion drained from Kim. "I can't change who my parents are."

Mitch lifted his head but turned his face to the side window. "No, you can't."

"Nor would I, even if it were possible," Kim added with a sharp edge on her voice. "That issue is never going to lose significance for you, is it?"

"How can it?" Mitch turned his head to look at her. "I guess I could quit my job."

"A slightly less than brilliant solution," Kim muttered impolitely. "In the first damned place, there is no issue. Putting it bluntly, the problem is only in your mind. My father—"

Mitch interrupted "You're not debating, you're accusing. You don't grasp the problem, so you think I shouldn't. It doesn't work that way, baby." There was a sarcasm in Mitch's voice. "We grew up differently, with different values and attitudes." The line of vehicles began moving onto the ferry. Mitch started the motor. "Have you tried at all to understand my side of it?"

"Of course I have." Kim was watching his profile, which conveyed intractable resolve. Once in place on the ferry, Mitch cut the engine. "Have you tried to understand mine?"

His expression remained grim. "I don't know that you have one."

"That's not fair! You've set your mind and won't even consider you might be wrong." Kim leaned closer to him. "Mitch, give the Armstrongs a chance. Let me arrange something, maybe a little dinner party with my folks. I guarantee you would like them."

"I already like them. Liking them isn't the issue." His glance contained a challenge. "Don't try to convince me that things wouldn't change if Sarge thought you and I were seeing each other. I'm doing good in the company, and I'm doing it on my own. I don't want you interfering with that, Kim."

Her eyes cooled. "In other words, you and I don't stand a chance."

Mitch looked at her for a long time and finally spoke in a voice that smacked of joyless resignation. "It's what I've been trying to tell you all along. I'm not saying I like it. If you were someone else..." His mouth clamped shut.

"Finish it!" Kim demanded, almost angrily. "If I were someone else, what would happen?"

Mitch's eyes flashed. "What do you think would happen?"

"You'd let yourself like me? Let me tell you something, Mitch. You liked me the moment we met! That's something no one can control. Either we like a person right away or we don't, and *you liked me!* I felt exactly the same about you, which you well know." Kim's temper was again pressuring her good sense. "What exactly are you afraid of?"

"Afraid?" Mitch bristled at the word. "I'm not afraid of anything. Don't interpret common sense as fear."

"What is so damned sensible about denial? That's what you're doing, you know, denying the most glaring, blatant truth I've ever run into."

"Look!" Mitch turned in the seat. "You're the one who can't handle denial. You saw me, you wanted me and you can't accept the fact that I didn't fall at your feet!"

Kim gasped. "That's a horrible thing to say! I'm no more attracted to you than you are to me, and I have never expected or wanted a man to fall at my feet."

The "debate" was getting cruel. Mitch washed his hand down his face, a weary gesture. "We're not communicating. I didn't mean to say that and I'm sorry." The ferry was moving. The day was waning, the date nearly over. It had been another mistake. He was more torn up than before, and so was Kim. This was not an argument either of them could win. If she accepted his point of view, they would never see each other again. If he accepted hers, he would feel like a damned gigolo, and that antiquated word had entered his vocabulary only recently.

"I'm sorry, too." There was a quaver in Kim's voice. She was afraid she was falling in love with Mitch, and it seemed that the more he retreated, the deeper she sank. Was that obstinacy, or was it an immutable fact and a curse that would haunt her for the rest of her life?

Frustration gripped her. Was there anything worse than a stubborn man? A man so entrenched in a ridiculous notion that he could see no alternatives? If she could only get him past the first huge hurdle. If just once he would admit his feelings without conditions....

They were both relieved when the ferry ride was over. They had fallen into an uncomfortable silence, certainly not the high point of the afternoon. Kim wondered if she shouldn't take off the vest he'd bought for her and hand it back to him with some kind of caustic remark. But she didn't want to hand it back, nor did she want any more anger between them.

Mitch drove directly to his apartment complex. The rain was again a fine drizzle, but the heavy cloud cover was causing a premature nightfall and it was getting dark. He left the motor running and looked at her.

"Thanks for the afternoon," he said quietly.

"Thanks for the vest," she returned just as quietly. And then she stopped thinking and analyzing and simply did what she wanted. It happened so quickly. One second she was sitting on the passenger side of the seat and the next she was sharing the driver's side with Mitch. It was so strange, because her sudden move apparently caught Mitch so off guard that he, too, reacted on impulse alone.

Whatever it was, his arms had lifted around her and she was plastered against him, her vest to his, her face in the open vee of his shirt, his warmth surrounding her, their hearts beating harder and in unison.

She sat there, stunned that he wasn't pushing her away, and then moaning softly, she snuggled closer. The muscles of his arms flexed and held her tighter. She could hear his raspy breathing, and feel it in her hair.

"Mitch...this isn't wrong," she whispered, finally raising her head to see his face.

He looked at her with dark, tormented eyes. "I've never wanted anyone more."

Her heart leapt with joy. "Nor I."

"Do you want to come in?"

"You know I do."

His face reflected an internal battle. "We'll be sorry tomorrow."

"I don't think so." She waited, anxiously, nervously, knowing that he was capable of changing directions in the blink of an eye. But the thought of going in with him, of having the evening, the night, together, lifted her to another plane. There must be something she could say right now to reassure him. Her mind raced, seeking the best words.

"We didn't ask for this kind of attraction, Mitch. I know I wasn't looking for it and I doubt that you were. It happened all on its own. We're not kids, and we're only human, aren't we? I'm not asking for commitment, and I'm sure you're not, either. Ask me in. I won't be sorry tomorrow, I promise, and if you are . . ."

His resistance was being overpowered by desire. She was right about one thing: he was only human. Groaning, he brought his mouth down on hers, silencing her, kissing her with the hunger that had built all afternoon. All day his gaze had rarely left Kim, and never had his thoughts deserted her. His body had been ready for this for so many hours, it was a wonder he hadn't ravaged her on that rocky beach.

He wasn't merely seeking pleasure from their kisses. He was driven by internal pressures and nearly beyond reason. She was like the light at the end of a long, dark tunnel. Each caress he bestowed, and each that he received, seemed to bring the light closer.

This time his mouth was open for her tongue. Within the momentum and energy of their wild kisses, they gasped for breath. His hands went beneath her new vest to the warmth of her body, to her breasts; her hands unbuttoned his shirt and reveled in his hot, bare skin.

A glimmer of sanity broke through Mitch's passion; they were outside, and though darkness was rapidly descending, it was rare when someone wasn't out and about in the large apartment complex.

"Come on," he growled raggedly, and switched off the motor, took the keys and then Kim's hand, opened the driver's door, got out and drew her out, as well.

He saw the dazed expression on her face. "My purse," she whispered.

Reaching back into the vehicle, he snagged her purse and put it in her hand. "Take your keys." He pressed them into her hand. With his arm around her, he steered her to his building. At the door of his apartment, he pulled his own keys from a pocket in his jeans, and then realized that his hand was shaking, and unlocking the door wasn't the mundane task that it usually was.

He pushed the door open and let Kim precede him. Entering behind her, he shut the door and pulled her into his arms. The apartment was darker than the outside, and he didn't turn on a light nor did Kim ask for one. All she did was melt into him, wrap her arms around his waist and lift her face for his kiss.

He was lost, totally and completely without constraints. His lips moved over her face. He pressed his hands against her hips and brought her closer, and every tiny remnant of common sense fled his mind.

Kissing her mouth, he pushed the vest from her shoulders. It fell to the floor, unnoticed. His own vanished next, then his shirt. With trembling fingers, he brought her T-shirt over her head and dropped it. In the twilight he could make out the glistening paleness of her skin and the demarcation of her bra. Kim herself flicked open the bra clasp, and Mitch felt his knees get weak at the sight of her full, lush bosom.

She crept back into his arms, and the sensation of her breasts against his bare chest was like an electrical shock. His kisses became rougher, hungrier. They strained together, hands roaming, skin tingling, desire mounting.

In unspoken agreement, they separated to get rid of their shoes and jeans, and then as though starved for contact, they rushed to find each other again. Their nudity was the final leap to intimacy. Mitch scooped her up off the floor and strode to the bedroom door, which Kim had left ajar after her curious inspection earlier. He kicked it open and unerringly walked to the bed, where he bent over and laid her down so her head was on a pillow.

Her arms stayed locked around his neck. Her breath feathered against his lips. "Do you have a condom?" she whispered.

"Yes."

It was the only words they'd spoken since he'd told her to take her keys. Neither had needed words. They were communicating on the most basic of levels, living a sexual fantasy, absorbed, rapt and completely in tune with each other.

Mitch took care of protection and returned to Kim's eager arms. He kissed her breasts and lingered at each to wet the nipple and suck gently. Her low moans of pleasure touched his soul, and a discordant thought flicked through his mind: he cared for her too much. This wasn't just a casual encounter, not for him, not for her.

But stopping wasn't an option. Getting off this bed unfulfilled and unsatisfied might kill him. Never had he been so driven, so led by primal passions. Nothing else seemed to matter, not his job, not Kim's parents, not his future, or hers or what might happen tomorrow. There was only now, this moment, and this beautiful, passionate, persistent lady, whose hands felt so delicious on his body, whose lips were the most exciting he'd ever tasted, whose voice, even in argument, seeped into his very cells. He felt like a reed in a pond, swayed and directed by much stronger elements, and maybe that was love. Maybe Kim Armstrong was the woman he was destined to love through eternity.

His moan was a combination of utter misery and the most profound pleasure of his life. "Mitch?" Kim whispered.

He kissed her, a coward's detour around controversy. But he couldn't say something distracting now, he just couldn't. When they both needed air, he broke the kiss and gulped a lungful, then slid down her body to press his mouth against her belly. The room was dark now and Kim was barely discernible. He didn't need to see, though, not to open her thighs and to kiss her most secret spot.

"Oh, Mitch." It was a low, tormented moan. She couldn't lie still. His mouth and tongue were hot and wet, a delectable sensation which uncoiled the tension in her body at a rapid rate. She urged him to move up again, to return to her arms, and when he complied, he gently mated their bodies.

It wasn't gentle for long. When he knew she was with him, he couldn't move slow and easy. He took her the way he had to, with strength and power and an overwhelming need to reach that golden light.

Her cries came at nearly the same moment as his own. As lovers they functioned perfectly, he realized with both elation and a vague but noticeable discomfort. He pushed the discomfort away—right now he could do nothing else—and rode the wave to its crest. When Kim silently asked for a kiss, he gladly accommodated her. At this moment he would do anything for her, climb mountains, swim oceans, walk barefoot on hot coals.

But then the kiss was over, the desire sated and the passion of the afternoon excitingly mollified. The room was dark and silent. Beneath him Kim was a small, soft mound, and he had no idea what to say to her. His mouth was suddenly dry with the reality of what he'd just done. The thought of hurting her was abhorrent, but how could he let her assume they had a future simply because he had temporarily lost his ability to reason?

He slowly raised his head and peered at her in the dark. What he heard from her, spoken softly, throatily, emotionally, nearly stopped his heart.

"Mitch, I think I'm falling in love with you."

Five

___

He couldn't answer, couldn't even *think* of an answer. Stiffly he moved across the bed. Then, getting off it, he felt his way to the closet and pulled out a pair of sweatpants, which he awkwardly but hastily struggled into. He practically ran from the bedroom to the bathroom.

Kim lay there with her heart thumping, wondering if he had heard her. If so, why hadn't he said something?

Mitch was only gone a few minutes, and when he returned she sat up and asked, "Is there a lamp by the bed?" She located it herself before Mitch could respond and switched it on. Light flooded the room. Blinking, Kim found Mitch over by the door. "Did you hear what I said?"

His eyes shifted to avoid hers. "I heard." Moving to his bureau, he opened a drawer and brought out a white undershirt.

The sudden viselike sensation around Kim's chest felt smothering. "Is that all you're going to say, that you heard?"

Mitch pulled the undershirt over his head. "I wish you hadn't said it."

Kim's stomach tensed. She'd gone too far again. Why did she keep doing that? Why, with Mitch, was she a different person than she was with anyone else?

But suddenly recalling her attempt to reassure Mitch in the car, when she'd jabbered that foolishness about not wanting a commitment, she lowered her eyes, chagrined. She sensed when he approached the bed, and moved over to give him room when he sat down. Obviously her mentioning the possibility of loving him had been a shock. She would be careful to stifle any such impulses in the future, though it seemed like the saddest thing she'd ever had to do. Right now her mind was teeming with things she would adore telling him, saying to him, sharing with him, and instead she had to pretend nonchalance over the most meaningful event of her life.

But she could do it. Someday he wouldn't retreat like this. They had made emotional headway today, whether he could admit it or not, and forcing Mitch into discomfiting discussions before he was ready could possibly do irreparable damage to their relationship.

Deliberately Kim put a teasing lilt into both her voice and expression. "You're great in the sack, Conover." When he only looked at her, obviously startled over the unexpected remark, she added, "You shock very easily, don't you?"

"I don't think you're experienced enough to make that sort of comment."

Was that disapproval in his eyes? Instantly defensive, Kim settled back on the pillow. "Maybe I am and maybe I'm not. Does my experience or lack thereof matter to you?"

It mattered a lot, but admitting it to himself was a far cry from saying as much to Kim. Instead he said, "You don't have to answer to me for anything."

"Well, of course not," Kim retorted rather sharply. Conversation with Mitch was close to impossible. But, hearing the bite in her voice and remembering that she had just decided to avoid controversy, she quickly smiled. "Let's agree not to disagree, okay?"

"That's fine with me." Uneasy with the topic in general, Mitch changed it. "Are you hungry?"

Kim's smile, though not entirely genuine, remained fixed. "Could be. What have you got to eat?"

"I don't know. I'll go see what's in the refrigerator."

"I'll help." Throwing back the blankets to get up, Kim saw his eyes widen. She honestly hadn't given her nudity a thought. They had made love in the dark, and Mitch hadn't really seen her naked until now. Her pulse speeded up, but she didn't move.

But then, he was in her way. Neither had he moved, and he was still sitting on the edge of the bed. And he was looking, intently, with a slightly staggered expression, as though he had never seen a naked woman before. Kim's chest was suddenly tight. "Enjoying the sights?" she asked huskily.

Mitch dampened his lips. "You are seriously beautiful."

His low, whispery voice shivered through Kim. She had never thought herself capable of exhibitionism, but lying there with Mitch's eyes heating up and devouring her was the most exciting thing she'd ever done. However much he fought their developing closeness, he wasn't able to deny himself her body!

It was a stunning thought. She had him here, in the bedroom. He wouldn't talk about love or commitment with her, but he would make love. Was that enough? Could she live with that sort of relationship? Kim's thoughts advanced. If she settled for a purely physical relationship, wouldn't long-term togetherness eventually break down Mitch's barriers and release his ridiculous inhibitions?

Whether that did or did not happen, did she have the strength of will to deny either of them what they had started here this evening?

She saw his tongue flick again—his mouth must feel dry. She saw the darkening of his eyes and the unmistakable renewal of desire on his face, heard the quickening of his breathing. And then he lifted his hand and laid it on her waist with an expression that told her he couldn't stop himself from touching her.

It was a sensually poignant moment and Kim reveled in it. She felt so much for Mitch, and she didn't need time—as he did—to recognize and acknowledge their need of each other for what it was. Looking into his eyes, she took his hand and slid it up to her breast. He needed no further direction. Raptly he began exploring the contours of her body, with both of his hands slowly smoothing and gliding over her bare skin.

"You are exquisite," he whispered, realizing vaguely that like *gigolo, exquisite* was a brand-new addition to his vocabulary. But it suited Kim's perfection, suited her proud breasts, tiny waist and slender hips, her sensual thighs, her creamy throat, her feminine feet and hands. She wasn't Sarge Armstrong's daughter now, she was merely a woman, and *merely* wasn't even half accurate. But because of her, he felt ten feet tall and powerful. Because of her he felt alive and soaring again, capable of astounding sexual feats, capable of great accomplishments.

"Kim..." *I want you...I want you.*

Her eyes contained the knowledge of the ages. Her voice was as soft as a falling rose petal. "Yes, Mitch?"

He stared for a moment, then grabbed the neck of his undershirt behind his head and yanked it off. Kim's heartbeat went wild. "Take off the rest, too," she whispered "Let me see all of you."

He stood up and slid the sweatpants down his legs, stepping out of them when they had bunched at his ankles. His body was magnificent, a laborer's body, taut, muscular, with black hair between his nipples and another black nest surrounding his sex.

She stared at his arousal, physically unable to lift her gaze. Then she said the same thing he had said to her. "You are seriously beautiful."

He gave a wry, short laugh and lay down beside her, supporting himself on one elbow to stay above her. With his eyes dark and smoldering, he slowly brought his head down to press his mouth to hers. Willingly, Kim's lips parted. If she had anticipated haste from Mitch, she was wrong. His kiss was rife with desire but languorous and leisurely. He tasted her lips, nipped at them with his teeth and wet them with the tip of his tongue.

"Oh, that's good," she whispered thickly, with her lashes lifting and falling and a glazed, dazed look in her eyes.

"Is this good, too?" He caressed her breasts, gently but freely, tracing their fullness and then teasing the nipples to rigidity.

"Very."

"And this?" His hand skimmed down her belly to the curls between her thighs. Knowingly, he parted her legs. Knowingly, he explored.

A moan whispered past her lips. "You know it is." Of her own volition she adjusted her position to give him more leeway. Maybe she couldn't mention love to Mitch, but she was thinking about it, thinking very hard and passionately. *You might shy away from talking about anything permanent between us, but I know you're falling in love with me, the same as I'm doing with you. I know it!*

Her own feelings roused her libido almost as much as Mitch's ardent attentions. Twisting slightly to free both her hands, she brought them to his chest. He kissed her lips, taking them with more hunger this time. Emboldened by passion, Kim dropped one hand to his arousal, and she felt a shudder pass through his body when she reached it and began her own exploration.

When she could speak, she whispered raggedly, "Do you like my touching you?"

"I like it. A lot."

His hoarse voice thrilled her. His hands thrilled her, his kisses, his body, his smell, everything about him.

But it could only go on for so long. Nearly crazed by desire, Mitch again used protection and moved between her thighs. His penetration brought tears to Kim's eyes. She clung and wept and nearly passed out from the power of her release. And she realized how vocal Mitch was in the final ecstasy when he shouted her name. *"Kim!"*

It was an emotional trip, an emotional aftermath. Weak and drained, with her mind barely working, Kim lay there, too sated to move.

Mitch moved first, finally raising his head to look at her. "Hi."

There was more tenderness in his voice and eyes than Kim had ever witnessed. "Hi," she returned softly, positive that not only was she seeing tenderness, she was seeing love, affection, affirmation and, yes, commitment.

Mitch smiled. "This could easily become a habit."

"My thoughts exactly," Kim whispered.

"Can you stay the night?"

She hesitated. Not once in her life had she spent a full night in a man's bed. For that matter, never had a man spent a full night in hers. She would like to stay. She would like to sleep in Mitch's arms and awaken in the morning snuggled close to him.

But how much dare she give him when he gave nothing more than his body? His cutting remarks about "an affair" flicked through her mind. Regardless of their perfection in bed, and regardless that she hoped for something permanent to come out of their lovemaking, to him this was only an affair and that's all it could ever be.

"I really can't," she said slowly, and seeing a shadow enter his eyes, added, "Maybe another night."

"Sure," he said casually. "Another night." With a slightly cynical grin, he untangled their bodies and slid from the bed.

Kim's heart began pounding. Maybe she hadn't handled that well. For a minute there, they had been on the same wavelength. With a rising anxiety, she watched him snag his sweatpants from the floor and disappear into the bathroom.

Wondering what she should do next, Kim worried a thumbnail with her teeth. Searching for a "next move" wasn't a pleasant exercise. Whatever came next should be

spontaneous after such incredible lovemaking. She should
be able to speak her thoughts; Mitch should be able to speak
his. They should communicate, exchange secrets, confidences, hold each other, make plans for their next date.

But...maybe she had pressured him too much already.
It was strange how Mitch affected her. Never had she been
so bold with another man. Never before had she acted as
pursuer with *any* man. Never, with any other man, had she
been the one to instigate a conversation about falling in love,
or even hinted at the subject of commitment.

Kim heaved a long sigh and threw back the blankets.
Apparently Mitch was dawdling in the bathroom, and since
she wasn't staying the night, she may as well get dressed.

Hurrying to the living room, Kim gathered her clothes off
the floor and dashed back to the bedroom to put them on.
She was dressed when Mitch returned with a towel around
his hips.

Sending him a smile, Kim went in search of her purse and
found it near the apartment's front door. "Okay if I use the
bathroom now?" she called.

"Go ahead," Mitch called back from the bedroom.

In the bathroom she brushed her hair, washed her face
and put on some makeup. It startled her to see sadness in her
eyes. She bit her lip. Vowing not to fall harder for Mitch
than he did for her had been a waste of time and effort. She
had fallen as hard as any woman ever had, and Mitch was
giving her nothing to hang on to. If she was really as smart
as she'd always thought, wouldn't she walk out of this
apartment and never come back?

For a long, introspective moment Kim thought about
telling Mitch goodbye, leaving and never doing one more
thing to bring them together. If an accidental meeting arose
she could sidestep it, and if he should take a notion to call
her again, she could be polite but distant.

Hastily she shoved her cosmetics into her purse. *That* was
a decision she couldn't make right now. She would tell Mitch
goodbye and leave, but the thought of crossing off any future meetings was just too painful.

He was standing in the middle of the living room when she walked in, wearing the sweatpants and undershirt. "Ready for some supper?" he asked.

Kim smiled. "I'm going to go home, but thanks for the offer."

"Kim..."

The shadow of unhappiness in his eyes and the grim set of his mouth tore through her. "Hey, don't look so stricken," she said lightly. "I'm fine. It's simply time to go."

"I didn't want this to happen." His voice conveyed misery. "I knew you'd end up hurt."

"Hurt? What makes you think I'm hurt?" The word focused her attention on the dull ache in her midsection. Yes, she was hurting, but would admission and discussion make that knot of frustration go away? She didn't think so. Mitch was still miles away from her own level of honesty, still hung up on her being his boss's daughter.

A wary glint had appeared in Mitch's eyes. "I hope you're not."

Kim slung the strap of her bag over her shoulder. "Why would I be hurt? I got what I wanted, didn't I?"

Mitch's eyes narrowed. "Did you?"

"You performed..."

"Stop it!" Scowling, Mitch advanced. "That kind of remark is out of character for you, and I don't like it."

"What makes you think you know me well enough to judge my character?" Her own anger surprised Kim. Apparently it had been brewing all afternoon and waiting for an opportunity to snap. "You don't know me. You won't *let* yourself know me." She took a calming breath. "Besides, Mitch, what you like isn't the only consideration. I'll say anything I want, anytime I want, and if it chafes your sensibilities, that's simply too bad. Goodbye."

Eyes wide and startled, Mitch watched her head for the front door. She had her hand on the knob when he said, "Kim!"

"Yes?" She turned.

"Don't leave like this."

"Like what, Mitch?"

Walking toward her, he scrubbed his hand across his mouth. "Upset . . . angry. Kim, I tried to warn you."

"Yes, you did." She studied the brooding contours of his face. "What's really bothering you, Mitch? Would you rather I crept away feeling guilty because we made love? I don't feel a dram of guilt, nor am I sorry it happened, but maybe I should pretend I do. Would a little pretense appease your own guilt? That's what you're suffering, isn't it? Guilt because you made love to your boss's daughter?" Kim rolled her eyes. "I still can't believe that *you* believe there's something wrong with you and I being together. Tell me this, Mitch, do you place our relationship in the criminal category? The sinful?"

"It's ethics, dammit! Don't you have any?"

"Oh, please," she drawled. "It's not my ethics you're questioning, it's my father's." She glared at him. "Isn't that true? Aren't you thinking that Dad would come unglued if he found out about us? He wouldn't, you know. I doubt very much that he would give it a moment of his time."

"Yeah, right."

Kim's chin lifted at his sarcasm. "You're wrong, Mitch, and if anything about you does hurt me, it's your stubborn refusal to consider more than one side of our situation." Kim's shoulders suddenly slumped. "I promised myself I wouldn't do this. Good night, Mitch. Call me if you feel like talking."

He stood in the doorway and watched her cross the lighted parking lot, weariness and defeat on his face. This wasn't fair, but then, what was? Life was one dose of reality after another. He'd learned that lesson young, and little had happened to alter that opinion. Daily living was a good job, if you were fortunate enough to have one, a few close friends, if you were lucky enough to have them, and struggling with dreams and aspirations, if you were still idealistic enough at almost-thirty to possess them. His and Kim's relationship had been doomed to failure from the first, which he had tried to make clear to her. Today shouldn't have happened. He should have maintained control.

After Kim's taillights had vanished, Mitch muttered a dark curse and stepped inside to slam the door shut. He could love Kim—maybe he already did—but thank God she hadn't stayed all night. By morning he probably would have been a simpering idiot and forgotten every standard he lived by.

Kim picked up the telephone in her studio. "This is Kim Armstrong. May I help you?"

"It's Julie Hildebrand, Kim. Listen, I ran across a photo of the most exquisite bedroom in a magazine. Everything is done in shades of white, and I've fallen in love with it. Do you think you could work up a proposal in white for my bedroom suite?"

"Certainly, Mrs. Hildebrand." Thus far, nothing she had presented to Julie Hildebrand had been exactly right. Kim had been wondering, in fact, if the lady knew her own mind. But if she had found something she truly liked, Kim was more than happy to try yet another proposal. "Do you have the magazine?"

"Right here in my hands."

"I'd like to see it. Could I stop by later today, Mrs. Hildebrand?"

"Come anytime, Kim. I plan to be home all day."

"See you later, then." Kim put down the phone. Looking at the mess on her desk, she groaned out loud. Stacks of fabric swatches, books of wallpaper samples, paint chips, color charts, client files and loose papers were everywhere. Ordinarily she kept her studio neat and tidy, but she wasn't functioning on all cylinders these days. Since last winter, when she'd been so busy with the Meridian models, she had, off and on, thought about hiring an assistant. But not to keep her desk clean, dammit!

Angry at herself for letting Mitch Conover turn her world upside down, Kim attacked the messy desk. All day Sunday she had listened for the phone, at first certain that he would call and then, by the end of the day, almost ill because she knew he wasn't going to. And he wouldn't call this week, either, because he was working in Olympia.

What kept her tense was the fear that he would never contact her again. He was just pigheaded enough to call it quits for them in his own mind, and leave her hanging. She had asked for trouble and she'd gotten it, and there was little comfort in hoping that he, too, was doing some suffering. There would be a modicum of satisfaction in seeing it with her own eyes, but what ploy could she use this time to bring them together?

Carrying a stack of trade journals to the bookcase on the studio's west wall, Kim heaved a wounded sigh. She disliked the role of pursuer, loathed it, in fact. But the thought of doing nothing brought crushing visions of regret for years to come. There had to be a way around Mitch's misguided attitude toward his job. Should she manipulate a social get-together for him and her parents? Not that it would be an easy feat, and what if Mitch despised her for it? But losing him over something so groundless was an abhorrent prospect.

If she felt nothing important from him, she wouldn't be so determined, she told herself. She did feel something important from Mitch, didn't she?

Blinking back tears, Kim finished clearing her desk. Then she began gathering items to prepare another presentation for Julie Hildebrand—swatches of fabrics in off-white, oyster white, pearl, snowy, everything she had in the studio even close to white. An hour later, with her service bag loaded, she turned on the answering machine, locked the studio and left.

Mitch's motel room was small, nondescript and impersonal. Stretched out in bed with his hands clasped behind his head, he stared at the shadowy ceiling. *Kim... Kim....*

She was all he thought about, whether working, eating, showering or trying to sleep. He knew that some of his crew were having beers in the motel lounge. They'd asked him to join them, but he felt as antisocial as he ever had in his life. Antisocial and miserable. Falling for the wrong woman was the pits. What the hell was going on with him? He couldn't have Kim Armstrong and that was that, so why couldn't he stop remembering how she felt in his arms? How she smelled? Tasted? Why dwell on a smile he should never see again, or on a voice he should never hear again?

It wasn't late. Pulling himself up, Mitch switched on the lamp and stared at the phone. He'd done the same damned thing every night he'd been in Olympia; stared at the phone, wondered, worried. This was the fourth night, Thursday. Tomorrow afternoon the crew would return to Seattle for the weekend. They would come back to Olympia on Monday morning to finish the job, which should be completed on Wednesday.

The phone sat there, silent and mocking Mitch. He wiped his mouth while raw nerves churned in his gut. Kim probably wasn't even home. With her open, aggressive personality, she had to have lots of friends and social engagements. She could be out with a man, laughing at his jokes, smiling her fabulous smile, letting him kiss her.

No! She wasn't kissing someone else, she wasn't! Mitch's hand jerked out and grabbed the phone. Before he could change his mind again, he punched nine for an outside line and then Kim's number.

She answered on the third ring. "Hello?"

Mitch cleared his throat. "Kim?"

"Mitch?"

"Yeah. How've you been?"

"Keeping busy. How about you?"

Mitch swung his feet to the floor. "The job's going fine. We should finish up next Wednesday."

"Will you be working through the weekend?"

"No. We'll go home for the weekend and come back on Monday."

"I see." Kim drew a breath. She was so glad he'd called she felt dizzy. What should she say? What would *he* say? A thousand words were in her mind, but every one of them could be interpreted wrong by Mitch.

"I'd like to apologize for not calling before this," Mitch said, his voice low in her ear. "I should have called...before this."

"I've been hoping you would," she said softly. "Better late than never, Mitch."

"Then you're not mad at me?"

"No, I'm not mad at you."

"When you left..."

"I know. I'm sorry. It's just that we feel so differently about...things."

"I can't change, Kim. I know you don't understand and it's always going to be between us, but I can't change. I wish I could. I wish...so much, but wishing is a kid's game and I haven't been a kid for twenty years."

Twenty years? At not quite thirty he could say he hadn't been a kid for twenty years? Kim frowned. "I'm not a kid, either, Mitch."

"I know you're not. No kid could ever do to me what you have, Kim."

Her breath caught in her throat. "What did I do, Mitch?"

"Turned me inside out. I think of you all the time."

Kim felt a dizzying joy. "That's not bad, is it, Mitch? I hope it isn't, because I think of you all the time, too."

"You do?"

"All the time, Mitch. I was thinking of you when the phone rang. Where are you calling from?"

"My motel room."

"Are you in bed?" The idea roughened her voice.

"I was. I'm sitting up now. What are you doing?"

"I had a bath and put on my nightie about an hour ago. But I can't go to sleep this early and I was going over some work I brought home from the studio." Kim's voice became more intimate. "Mitch, I'm so glad you called." *Say something about the weekend, please! Say that we should see each other. Tell me you want us to see each other.* She could say it, very easily. But she was trying so hard not to push him again.

"Kim . . . I don't know what to do about us."

There was so much misery in his voice, Kim's heart ached for him. "What do you want to do, Mitch? Not what you think you should do, but what you want. Tell me, please."

She heard him draw a ragged breath before he said, gruffly, "I think you already know what I want."

"I know what *I* want, Mitch," she said sadly. "I can only guess at what goes on in your mind." There was a pause. "I'm making you terribly unhappy, aren't I?"

"No!" Another pause. "Not you, Kim. You're not making me unhappy. Circumstances are doing that."

"Those circumstances would only be smoke without my involvement, Mitch." Kim sighed. The circumstances were only smoke *with* her involvement, some kind of ghostly specter in Mitch's mind. What in God's name had occurred in his lifetime to make him so wary and so set against a relationship with a woman that also touched on his employer?

She couldn't let it alone, not when she sensed that he was going to back off again at any second and probably startle her with a quick goodbye.

"Mitch, you have to make an effort to alter your opinion of my father's outlook. Mother invited me to dinner on Saturday night. It's Dad's birthday, and . . ."

Almost harshly, Mitch interrupted. "No, Kim. Don't ask me to do that. I'm not going to Sarge's on the shirttail of your invitation. Besides, if it's a birthday party, it's a family affair."

"It's not only family. There'll be others there."

"Close friends, I'm sure. No, forget it. Look, I've got to go."

"Go where?" He was wriggling away again, and the need to grab him by the shoulders and shake the very breath out of him was so strong and pungent, Kim had to grit her teeth.

"I mean, it's time to say good-night."

She exhaled soundly, hoping he heard the exasperation she was feeling. "I suppose it is. Well, however frustrating it was, I'm still glad you called."

"Was talking to me frustrating, Kim?"

"Damned right it was, and don't tell me it didn't frustrate you, too, because I know better. Good night, Mitch."

After she hung up, partly angry, partly grief stricken, Kim remembered something she had meant to tell Mitch: he had left his cowboy hat in the back of her car.

But maybe her forgetfulness had been a fateful oversight. Just maybe that mundane article was the means to another meeting with Mitch. For certain, *he* wasn't racking *his* brain to come up with one!

Six

Kim arrived at her parents' home at six on Saturday evening. Hearing the sound of voices and laughter at the back of the house, she brought her gift inside, said hello to Lois in the kitchen and promptly went out to the patio to join the party.

Sara and Sarge were passing out canapés and drinks. They called out an enthusiastic hello, and Kim went directly to her father to kiss his cheek. "Happy birthday, Dad."

He gave her an enthusiastic one-armed hug. "Thanks, baby. Did you see who's here?"

"Who?" Kim smiled at the guests, three couples, she saw, all good friends of her folks. And then her eyes widened. "Scot! Good heavens, is that really you?" Bounding forward, she ran into Scot Taylor's open arms.

"Hi, Kim."

"You old thing, you! Whatever brought you home from California?"

Grinning, Scot stepped back. "Just a spur-of-the-moment visit, Kim. Dad and Mother were thrilled to impose my presence on Sarge's birthday party, as you might have guessed."

Kim laughed. Seeing her lifelong friend was like catching a refreshing glimpse of childhood. The Taylors and the Armstrongs had been fast friends for longer than Kim could remember, and she and Scot had literally grown up in each other's company.

"So, how's the doctoring business?" she inquired teasingly. Scot was a pediatrician in the Los Angeles area, and doing very well, she knew from reports that Sara was always happy to pass on from Scot's mother. It was no secret that the two mothers had hoped years ago that their offspring would develop more than friendly feelings for each other.

It hadn't happened. Kim adored Scot—he was the big brother she'd never had—and they had experimented with kissing and fooling around a little in their teens. But that's as far as their relationship had ever gone. They were good friends and always would be, and that was the extent of it.

"The doctoring business is terrific," Scot replied with a twinkle in his gray eyes. "So is the decorating business, I've heard."

"I'm sure you have," Kim said with amused wryness. Her expression changed. "It's great to see you. You look wonderful. Healthy, happy and . . . rich!" She laughed again. Scot Taylor was a handsome man, tall and long-legged with a warm smile and gorgeous blond hair. "I know you're still single, but how come some little gal hasn't reeled you in yet?"

"Well . . . that might happen very soon now." Scot sent a glance to his mother and dad. "Keep that to yourself, okay? I'm planning to tell them about it this weekend, but I'd just as soon not start answering questions right this minute, if you get my drift."

"I get it, loud and strong."

"Here, honey." Sarge came up and pressed a tall glass into Kim's hand. He grinned at Scot. "It's still club soda with a twist of lime. This weird child of mine never did learn to appreciate the flavor of good liquor.''

They all laughed. Sarge liked his drinks, usually Scotch, and he also indulged in cigars when Sara wasn't close enough to object to the smoke and odor.

Sarge moved off. "I'd better say hello to your folks and the others," Kim murmured to Scot.

"We'll talk later, okay?"

"Count on it." Kim started away and stopped. "Are you going to be here for a while?"

"Only until tomorrow night, Kim. My plane leaves at eight."

She nodded. "Too bad. I was hoping we might spend an evening together."

"Not this trip, Kim, sorry."

She smiled at him, rather nostalgically, and wandered away to speak to the other guests.

The party was a success. The food was wonderful, and Sarge had a great time opening his gifts, most of which were in fun and caused a lot of hilarity. When the festivities were winding down, Scot approached her. "Let's take a walk."

"Gladly."

It was dark beyond the yard lights and they strolled along slowly. "Apparently you've met someone important," Kim said quietly.

"I think she is, Kim. Her name's Candace. She's a nurse in the pediatrics ward of one of the hospitals I'm associated with. A wonderful woman."

"You're in love with her."

"Head over heels."

Kim stopped and faced him. "How do you know?"

He studied her face in the dark. "That's a strange question."

"I really need to know, Scot. You sound so certain, and how can you be? How can *anyone* be that certain?"

"Hey, sounds like you might've run into someone who's got you confused on the subject."

"I have and I am." Kim gave a short laugh. "I'm falling deeper every day and he. . . ."

"What is it, Kim? What's wrong?"

"He . . . works for Dad."

"And?"

It came tumbling out. "He has this peculiar idea that he can't work for Dad and see me, too. Isn't that crazy?" They started walking again. "I don't know how to deal with it. We've gotten quite close. . . in some areas. . . and, yet, there's this frightening wall between us."

"That's tough," Scot said, sounding sympathetic. "I don't know what to tell you, Kim. What do Sarge and Sara think about it?"

"They don't know. I met him right here, when he came for dinner one evening, but neither of them know we ever saw each other again." Kim stopped again. "They wouldn't care, Scot," she said rather defensively. "Do you think they would care? Why would they?"

"Simmer down, Kim. I doubt very much that they'd object, but if you're so certain, why haven't you told them?"

"Why haven't you told your folks about Candace?"

Scot grinned, a little sheepishly. "The perfect rebuff. You're right. It's no one else's business until you know it's serious."

Looking off across the dark yard, Kim sighed. She couldn't find another word that fit so aptly as "serious." Her and Mitch's relationship was probably the most serious of her life, or it could be if he would lighten up and let it reach its potential.

It was nearing midnight when the last guest had gone. Kim said good-night to her folks, got in her four-wheeler and pointed it toward home.

But after a few miles she made a right turn and took another direction. In fifteen minutes she was driving slowly through Mitch's apartment complex. His pickup was parked near his unit, and she pulled into the next open space and turned off the ignition.

Her heart was pounding madly. He would probably be irritated by a midnight visit, but on the other hand, maybe he would be thrilled.

"Damn," she mumbled, despising what was becoming too many bouts of vacillation. Was she going to meekly accept Mitch's attitude? While pursuing a man wasn't common practice for her, neither was so much ambiguity.

She would knock on his door, and if he didn't like it, she would hand him his hat and leave.

Grabbing the hat, Kim quickly got out, quietly closed the door so as not to disturb the silent compound and made her way to Mitch's door. Instead of knocking, she pushed on the doorbell button.

The buzzing within the apartment made her wince, but a doorbell was supposed to be intrusive, and how else would she wake him?

She heard movement inside and waited for the door to open. Instead, she heard, "Who is it?"

"It's me, Mitch, Kim."

The door opened a mere crack. Mitch peered through the narrow opening. "Do you know what time it is?"

"Midnight," she said calmly, belying the butterflies in her stomach. "I have your hat."

"I didn't know you had it."

"You left it in my car." The door didn't open. "Don't you want it?"

There was a pause. "Kim, this isn't a good idea. I'll get it some other time."

"Take it now," she said coldly. Damn him! He wasn't even going to open the door wide enough for her to push the hat at him.

She heard his sigh. "Just a minute. I'm not dressed."

The door remained ajar, but Mitch disappeared. Gathering her courage, Kim pushed it open and stepped in. The apartment was dark; he hadn't turned on any lights.

"Mitch?"

"I'm in the bedroom. Give me a minute."

She could hear him fumbling around for some clothes, and she drew a quick breath, closed the door and headed for the bedroom. In the doorway she stopped. Mitch was a shadowy form in the dark. "Don't dress."

"What?"

"I asked you not to get dressed."

"Why not?"

"Take a wild guess," she said, her voice husky and not overly strong. She was doing it again, challenging him, daring him, and she couldn't seem to stop herself. Was this love, or was it insanity?

"Kim, dammit..."

To her ears he sounded helpless, a little short of breath. "Do you really want me to leave?" she whispered.

"I'm still half asleep," he mumbled.

She walked over to him. "We agreed on another night."

"Another night?"

"We agreed last weekend that I would stay all night at another time, didn't we?"

"And this is that night?"

"I'd like it to be." Inching closer to his warmth, she put her hands on his chest. "I want you, Mitch. I want you so much I ache from it." Her breath caught as her hands moved downward. "You're completely naked."

"It's how I sleep." He groaned deep in his throat when she touched him intimately. "Kim...you shouldn't be here."

"And the sun shouldn't rise nor the moon set," she whispered raggedly. "I don't seem able to control myself anymore, Mitch. If there was some way to get you out of my system, I'd do it, but I think what I've caught is a permanent condition. Do you think I like chasing a man who doesn't want me?"

"My God, it isn't that I don't want you!" The way she was holding him, she had to know exactly how much he did want her. Eluding her hands would be physically simple, just one backward step, but his will had totally vanished. Standing in the dark with her so close and inhaling her scent in huge draughts was more than enough ammunition to destroy any and all resistance he felt in saner moments.

He quit trying to do the right thing and brought his hands up to her upper arms. Jerking her forward, he found her lips with his, and then everything went crazy. They kissed hungrily, wildly, writhed together, moved and sought and gasped and moaned. Kim was wearing a skirt, and Mitch worked it up.

"I wasn't sure you'd be home," Kim whispered between kisses.

"I wasn't until about an hour ago." Mitch's voice was thick, his words guttural. His mind was spinning too fast to land on anything sensible. She was here, in his dark bedroom, wanting him, needing him, and right now nothing else had any substance.

Under her skirt he went into her panties. Her responsive moan fired his desire. Touching her was incredible. His affection and need for this particular lady exploded, and hastily he began undressing her.

Together they got rid of her clothes—her skirt and blouse, her bra and panties. He stroked her bare skin and kissed her mouth, her throat, her breasts, while her kisses fell wherever they landed, his lips, his chest, his throat. The emotion in Kim's system was so huge and overwhelming, her eyes began dripping tears. Nothing in her life had prepared her for this kind of hunger, nor had she ever missed it. How could she have when she hadn't known it truly existed?

She knew now, and nothing would ever be the same for her. Without Mitch, sunny days would seem cold and gray. Without Mitch, everything she had previously enjoyed doing would be dull and insipid, colorless, unexciting.

He was her excitement. He made her feel alive. With him her blood ran hot and fast, and she felt her own femaleness, reveled in it. How could she walk away now? And how could he, when he told her in every way but vocally that he felt the same about her?

With a few stumbling steps they fell to the bed, their arms and legs tangled, their bodies closely joined. Their kisses were breathy and brief. Neither of them could touch the other enough. Kim's fingertips seemed sensually sensitized as they roamed his hot skin, and his caresses increased her longing to the intolerable stage.

"Mitch...my love," she whispered raggedly, bringing his head down for a kiss of utter desperation.

He moved to lay in the cradle of her thighs, and when neither could bear the delicious torture another moment, he slid into her heat. Her sigh contained not only pleasure but contentment that he was where he belonged. There was something so very right about the two of them joined and making love. Nothing nor no one would ever convince Kim that they weren't destined to be together, and no damned job was going to ruin what they had. Not while she drew breath and could think and do something about it. If that meant boldness and creativity from her, so be it, but she was not going to lose Mitch!

There was a savagery to their lovemaking that hadn't been present during their first time together. Mitch wasn't as gentle as he'd been the weekend before, but his emotions were so torn up and jagged, and they came through in his powerful thrusts and hard, demanding kisses.

His fierceness excited Kim to new heights. She locked her legs around his hips and gave him everything she was and ever could be. If Mitch was where he belonged, so was she. There was not another man on the globe for her. She had met her soulmate, her lover for life, her husband-to-be, the father of her unborn children, and it was enough at the present that *she* knew it. Eventually so would Mitch, or rather, eventually he would admit what he already *had* to know.

Mitch mumbled something she hadn't caught. "What did you say?" she whispered.

He never stopped moving. "I'm crazy about you."

Kim's pulse went wild with joy. "I know, darling, I know." Her emotions nearly erupted in a spate of loving words, but judiciously she eluded the impulse. It was much wiser to wait for him to mention love and a future together:

she would not repeat the mistake she had made last weekend.

But then he said something else. "Or maybe I'm just crazy."

Before Kim could assimilate that disturbing comment, Mitch's passion had expanded to the final stage. She went with him, reached for the ultimate ecstasy and attained it with gasps and a blinding pleasure.

Breathless, she went limp, as Mitch did. He lay still until his breathing leveled out, then abruptly he rolled to the bed. "I didn't use a condom."

Kim's eyes had been closed in complete and utter satisfaction, and they jerked open. Haste to get out of bed made her awkward, and she stumbled in the dark. "Turn on the lamp."

Mitch sat up and switched on the bedside lamp. Without looking at him, Kim hurried away to the bathroom. But he'd seen the look of panic on her face, and his mouth set into a thin, grim line. That's all he needed now, Kim pregnant. His boss's daughter pregnant because he couldn't say no to her. How would he explain *that* to Sarge?

He glanced at the clock on the bed stand: 1:15 a.m. Stacking the pillows, he lay back wearily and shut his eyes. Yes, he was crazy about Kim, and yes, he was also just plain bonkers. She was the woman he wanted, the only woman. He couldn't justify it, couldn't explain it, couldn't accept it, but that's how it was. When she crooked her finger, he responded.

Even with his eyes closed, his expression become wry. She'd done a lot more than crook her finger. She'd come here at midnight, followed him to the bedroom in the dark and then her hands . . . her hands on him . . .

"Mitch?"

He opened his eyes. Kim was standing next to the bed, wrapped in a towel. Her hair was tossed and tumbled around her flushed face, and she had never looked more beautiful.

He lifted the blankets in invitation. Her lips shaped a small smile, and she dropped the towel and crawled in to snuggle against him. "Turn out the light," he said quietly.

Reaching out, Kim complied. Then she settled against him again. "I'm happy, Mitch, so very happy," she whispered.

"If you got pregnant tonight, you won't be so happy."

"I didn't get pregnant."

"You can't be sure."

"Yes, I can. It's the wrong time of the month." She wasn't as positive as she sounded, but what's done is done and there was little point in alarming Mitch with what-ifs. She raised her head slightly. "Would you like an explanation?"

"No."

She nestled close again. "Good." Beneath the blankets, her hand moved to his waist. "Your skin is hot and as smooth as satin. Right here, that is. Higher it's different, and lower..." She tested the lower territory and smiled. "Down here it's hot and...soft."

"It won't be soft for long if you keep that up," he growled.

"I was talking about your skin!"

"Yeah, right." Deliberately he took her hand and returned it to his waist. "That's much safer."

"You'd rather sleep."

"I'm tired. Aren't you tired?"

Kim stifled a yawn. "Yes, but sleeping seems like such a waste of time."

Wryly Mitch gave his head a slight shake. "Kim, Kim, what am I going to do with you?" He became deadly serious. "What am I going to do *about* you?"

"You said you were crazy about me," she whispered, and then bit her lip. "I guess, though, you began wondering if you weren't just crazy."

"I'm still wondering."

"Falling for someone doesn't make you crazy, Mitch."

"Falling for someone you know you have no right to is not exactly the act of a sane and sensible person, Kim."

Alarmed, Kim frowned. "You have every right to fall for me. I gave you that right at our first . . . no, our second meeting."

"But your permission isn't the only consideration."

"It should be. How you and I feel is all that matters, Mitch. The rest of the world could disapprove and it wouldn't affect—"

"Don't be naive, Kim." He'd spoken sharply, and he heaved a wary sigh almost immediately. "Let's not get into that tonight. I don't feel like arguing." He didn't. Lying there with Kim in his arms, his body relaxed and his mind drowsy, arguing any issue seemed only obtrusive. "Let's get some sleep."

Kim inhaled slowly, a long breath that she also released slowly. It was getting late and sleeping was only sensible. But she felt so close to Mitch right now, way beyond the obvious—close in spirit, in emotions. And talking in the dark was so incredibly pleasant. "This feels right, doesn't it?" she whispered. "Being together like this?"

"It feels great, but . . ."

There was always a "but" with Mitch, and it saddened Kim. He was as cozily situated as she was, as physically contented, as emotionally involved, and he still clung to reservations. If it was all up to her, tonight would be the first night of the rest of their lives. They would talk about loving each other, about permanency, about growing old together. She sighed longingly, wishing for things that would probably turn Mitch's hair gray.

She started to speak again and realized he was asleep. Sighing, she snuggled deeper into the crook of his arm and the bedclothes. At least she had tonight.

Drinking her breakfast coffee with Mitch at his small dining table the next morning was a high point, Kim acknowledged only to herself. He still looked sleepy; his eyes weren't completely open yet. Her smile wasn't exactly smug, but unquestionably her marvelously mellow feeling was because she was the reason he hadn't gotten in a solid eight hours of rest last night. He had reached for her twice after falling asleep the first time. His enormous sexual appetite for her was gratifying, a most welcome sensation. In plain language, Mitch was in love with her. She knew it as well as she knew anything, and the knowledge created a wonderful peace in her soul that she was certain would survive any and all hurdles.

"Let's do something fun today," she suggested brightly over her cup.

His gaze connected with hers. "I'm committed for the day."

Disappointment mingled with disbelief. Kim lowered her cup. "You are?"

He could invite her along, Mitch realized with a developing frown. His friends wouldn't mind at all if he brought a date to the day-long barbecue and pool party planned in the backyard of Jack and Sue Dain's new home. Jack was a member of Mitch's crew at work, and just recently he and Sue had bought their first house, which included, to their delight, a small swimming pool within their fenced yard. They were throwing the party to show off their new house and had invited everyone in the crew.

But just how would he introduce Kim? *Hey, gang, this lady is the boss's daughter!* Mitch's skin actually crawled at the thought. He could already see the sly glances and knowing expressions, and hear the wisecracks. Even if he could bear the flak, he couldn't expose Kim to it.

"I have other plans," he said stiffly.

"I see," Kim said in a very small voice.

"In fact..." Mitch checked his watch. "I'm going to have to get going. I have to be there at noon."

Feeling like a discard of some sort, Kim set her cup on the table. "Is it business or pleasure?"

"It's a promise, Kim."

Was it another woman? Kim died a little inside. Mitch was bound to have women friends, women who weren't related to his boss, women who didn't barge into his apartment in the middle of the night. She was too brazen, too pushy, and the aftermath might hurt, but didn't she deserve it?

Her chin came up. "Well, don't let me keep you."

"Don't get mad."

Kim got to her feet. "I wouldn't dream of it."

Mitch rose from his chair. "You're mad right now."

How could she deny it when even her fingernails were sizzling? But a fight was the last thing they needed, and she gritted her teeth in an effort to hold back the anger.

"I'll get my things." Kim strode from the room. Her "things" consisted solely of her purse, as she was already wearing the clothes she had arrived in at midnight.

Mitch followed her to the bedroom. Kim took a second to peer at herself in the mirror above the bureau. The night was written all over her face. She looked, she thought resentfully, like the morning after.

Swinging around abruptly, she faced Mitch. "Well . . . it was fun while it lasted."

"Just stop it," he said gruffly. "My plans for today don't take one damned thing away from last night."

"Then last night meant something to you?" She sounded belligerent.

"You know it did."

Kim rolled her eyes. "Please don't start telling me what I know again. If you could crawl into my brain and grasp what I do know, you just might get the shock of your life."

"That works both ways, Kim."

"Meaning your thoughts would shock me?"

Mitch looked away for a moment, finally returning guarded eyes to her. "We just don't connect, do we?"

Kim drew a startled, shaky breath. "We're not single-minded on everything, but we do connect, Mitch." Her voice weakened. "Please don't disagree."

"We connect in bed, Kim." He was speaking gently. "I don't want to keep hurting you, but that's how it always ends up. What're we going to do about it?"

Her laugh was brief and unsteady. "I suppose we have two options. Stop seeing each other or don't stop. I vote for the second." She didn't want to hear his vote, and she began moving toward the outside door. "So long, Mitch. See you around." If she didn't sound nonchalant, it wasn't for want of trying.

Her bravado touched him deeply, creating an ache in his gut. "Kim . . ." She turned with her hand on the doorknob. "I'll call, okay?"

Her smile was slightly watery. "Yes, okay." *When? When will you call? This evening? Next week?* "You'll be leaving in the morning to finish the Olympia project?"

"Yes, in the morning." And just like that, he knew he couldn't let her leave like this. Taking the few steps between them, he plunged his hand under her hair and cupped the back of her neck. His mouth brushed hers, softly, tenderly, then settled upon it for a real kiss.

She let go of her purse and wrapped her arms around him, leaning into him, kissing him back with all of the passion he had aroused within her since their very first meeting. She felt his arms drop around her, and he held her in a fierce, intense way, while their kisses intensified.

Breathlessly they looked at each other. Love and affection and a wild desire rode the path of their gazes. Easily they could return to the bedroom and make love throughout the day. Each knew it, each was thinking it.

Mitch slowly lowered his arms. She smiled weakly. "I'll call," he repeated huskily.

"Goodbye," she whispered. "Have . . . a good day."

"You, too."

Oddly, driving home Kim's vision was free of tears. The ache in her soul was so profound and earthshaking, she couldn't even cry. What would it take to change Mitch's outlook? Dear God, was she just so in love herself that she was imagining Mitch's feelings? Never had she visualized love as a physically painful emotion, and what kind of prolonged hell had she sentenced herself to with Mitch? Much more of this and she would be a raving lunatic.

If she had any sense at all, she would vote for the first option she had mentioned.

Apparently her good sense had been replaced by love.

How sad.

Seven

———

"Kim, I love your presentation. Let's do it." The caller was Julie Hildebrand, gushing over the package Kim had put together for an all-white bedroom. "When can you get started?"

Kim smiled faintly. Apparently Mrs. Hildebrand had forgotten all about "durable." Not that the white fabrics wouldn't hold up for years. But, as Kim had seen so many times, once a client found the exact look she wanted for a room, other factors lost importance.

"Right away," Kim replied. "I have three of the fabrics in my own inventory, Mrs. Hildebrand. The other two will have to be ordered, but shouldn't take more than a few weeks to arrive. I can have the upholstery company pick up your love seats tomorrow morning. The lampshades..." On and on went the recitation, the plans, the myriad details, encompassing wall coverings, draperies, upholstery and a magnificent white satin bedspread. Everything would be made-to-order, attuned uniquely to Julie Hildebrand's personal taste. Completed, the master suite would be a work of art, a job to be proud of.

But Kim wasn't feeling particularly proud of herself on any level these days. Her own behavior was a disruptive specter, intruding on her work, her rest and every other aspect of daily life. Telling herself that falling in love was a logical reason for losing touch with one's principles helped at times, but that argument didn't quite cut it in moments of complete honesty. She had chased Mitch until his confusion had hurt them both, and however she tried to gloss over the facts, they remained glaring and painful.

Mitch had called from Olympia on Monday evening.

"Hello, Kim."

"Hello, Mitch."

"Everything all right?"

"Everything's fine." A lie. Everything was not all right. The constant turmoil in her stomach, for instance. And the ghostly presence of deeply rooted remorse.

"I'm pretty sure we'll be here until the weekend. We had an equipment breakdown today, which stalled the project. Anyway, I've been doing some thinking, and I'd like us to meet to talk. How about Friday night?"

"You're missing a lot of your classes, aren't you?" Kim said quietly.

"Can't be helped. I'll make them up. What about Friday?"

"Friday is fine with me. Come to my place, Mitch. We can do our talking here."

"I'll be there around seven."

Kim had a little doubt about the subject matter of that inevitable chat, but when Mitch started insisting they stop seeing each other once and for all, he was in for a big surprise. Her mind was made up. Not only was she going to agree, she was going to apologize for making his life miserable. How many ways did a man have to say he wasn't interested before a woman caught on? Yes, he would make love with her, but an overwhelming sexual attraction did not necessarily mean anything more.

It was a harsh concept for Kim to accept, especially when she had truly fallen in love and knew she would hurt for a long time because of Mitch Conover. But, obviously, there was someone else in his life. What other reason could he have for ending Sunday so abruptly? Wouldn't he have explained an ordinary, impersonal commitment for the day?

"I'll stay closely in touch, Mrs. Hildebrand. Goodbye for now." With an inner sigh, Kim put down the phone. She had to force herself to pick it up again a few minutes later, but ordering those fabrics for the Hildebrand job was essential.

By Friday, Kim was a bundle of nerves. Mitch had called again on Wednesday evening, but she had been out on an appointment and he'd left a message on her answering machine. "Hi. This is Mitch. Nothing important. See you Friday night." Very brief, very impersonal. If he had nothing important to say, why had he called?

She forced a bowl of soup down around five-thirty just so her empty stomach wouldn't growl while they were talking. Then she rushed to the bathroom for a shower and shampoo, fully intending to be ready and waiting when he arrived at seven. Perversely she took great pains with her makeup and put on her most becoming sundress. The weather had been downright hot the whole week, and she had spent two mornings getting a light tan, which was all she ever allowed herself.

Dressed and ready, she took a rather calculating look at herself in a full-length mirror. The dress was colorful, a bold floral print in blues and greens, and the narrow straps curved enticingly over her bare shoulders. Her makeup was perfect, as was her hair. She had never looked better.

Her desire to look her best was only normal, she told herself, though a nagging little voice in the back of her mind seemed to relish accusing her of flaunting her best side to aggravate Mitch. Maybe it was true. Maybe she hoped he would do some suffering while looking her in the eye and telling her that he was never going to see her again.

FREE BOOKS!

FREE GIFT!

PLAY THE "LUCKY 7" SLOT MACHINE GAME !

AND YOU CAN GET FREE BOOKS PLUS A FREE GIFT!

NO COST! NO OBLIGATION TO BUY! NO PURCHASE NECESSARY!

PLAY "LUCKY 7" AND GET FIVE FREE GIFTS!

HOW TO PLAY:

1. With a coin, carefully scratch off the silver box at the right. Then check the claim chart to see what we have for you—FREE BOOKS and a gift—ALL YOURS! ALL FREE!

2. Send back this card and you'll receive brand-new Silhouette Desire® novels. These books have a cover price of $3.25 each, but they are yours to keep absolutely free.

3. There's no catch. You're under no obligation to buy anything. We charge nothing—ZERO—for your first shipment. And you don't have to make any minimum number of purchases—not even one!

4. The fact is thousands of readers enjoy receiving books by mail from the Silhouette Reader Service™ months before they're available in stores. They like the convenience of home delivery and they love our discount prices!

5. We hope that after receiving your free books you'll want to remain a subscriber. But the choice is yours—to continue or cancel, anytime at all! So why not take us up on our invitation, with no risk of any kind. You'll be glad you did!

© 1990 HARLEQUIN ENTERPRISES LIMITED

This beautiful porcelain box is topped with a lovely bouquet of porcelain flowers, perfect for holding rings, pins or other precious trinkets — and is yours absolutely free when you accept our no risk offer!

DETACH AND MAIL CARD TODAY

PLAY "LUCKY 7"

**Just scratch off the silver box with a coin.
Then check below to see the gifts you get.**

YES! I have scratched off the silver box. Please send me all the gifts for which I qualify. I understand I am under no obligation to purchase any books, as explained on the back and on the opposite page.

225 CIS ASXF
(U-SIL-D-06/95)

NAME

ADDRESS   APT.

CITY   STATE   ZIP

7 7 7	**WORTH FOUR FREE BOOKS PLUS A FREE PORCELAIN TRINKET BOX**
♣ ♣ ♣	**WORTH THREE FREE BOOKS**
● ● ●	**WORTH TWO FREE BOOKS**
♠ ♠ ♣	**WORTH ONE FREE BOOK**

Offer limited to one per household and not valid to current Silhouette Desire® subscribers. All orders subject to approval.

© 1990 HARLEQUIN ENTERPRISES LIMITED   **PRINTED IN U.S.A.**

Accepting free books places you under no obligation to buy anything. You may keep the books and gift and return the shipping statement marked "cancel". If you do not cancel, about a month later we'll send you 6 additional novels, and bill you just $2.44 each plus 25¢ delivery and applicable sales tax, if any.* That's the complete price, and—compared to cover prices of $3.25 each—quite a bargain! You may cancel at any time, but if you choose to continue, every month we'll send you 6 more books, which you may either purchase at the discount price...or return at our expense and cancel your subscription.

*Terms and prices subject to change without notice. Sales tax applicable in N.Y.

If offer card is missing, write to: Silhouette Reader Service, 3010 Walden Ave., P.O. Box 1867, Buffalo, NY 14269-1867

BUSINESS REPLY MAIL

FIRST CLASS MAIL   PERMIT NO. 717   BUFFALO, NY

POSTAGE WILL BE PAID BY ADDRESSEE

SILHOUETTE READER SERVICE
3010 WALDEN AVE
PO BOX 1867
BUFFALO NY 14240-9952

NO POSTAGE
NECESSARY
IF MAILED
IN THE
UNITED STATES

But then, she wasn't all that positive about his reasoning now, was she? Until Sunday, she'd believed that his job was the only factor hindering his affection. Sunday hinted at something else, and the only thing that made any sense was another woman.

Standing very still at the mirror, Kim saw the shadow of unhappiness in her eyes. Her feelings were coming through. She could primp till doomsday and her eyes would still reflect her inner dejection.

The doorbell rang. Kim jumped. Mitch was right on time. Taking one more quick look in the mirror, Kim pasted on a smile and hurried through the condo to open the door. A small satisfaction developed within her when Mitch's eyes warmed with admiration.

"Hi. Come in." Kim stepped back. Her own admiration was buried beneath an impassive voice. He looked great, as he always did, tall and handsome and too damned sexy. His clothes were tan cotton slacks and a white knit shirt, ordinary garments that appeared special because they were adorning a perfect body.

"Thanks." Mitch stepped into the foyer.

Kim closed the door and led the way to the living room. "Sit down. Would you like a cold beer?"

"Sure, thanks."

"Be right back." Forcing herself to walk naturally, Kim left Mitch in the living room and went to the kitchen and the refrigerator. Her heart felt as heavy as a lump of lead. This situation might be her own fault, but having no one else to blame wasn't especially comforting. Besides, was it really her fault that she'd fallen for the wrong guy? Had she really had anything to say about it?

She returned with a beer for Mitch and a glass of ice tea for herself. "Sit down," she repeated.

Mitch sank to the sofa. Kim took a chair. They sipped from their drinks. Mitch's gaze lingered on her. "You look beautiful in that dress."

"Thank you." The compliment was gratifying, but Sunday was still stuck in Kim's craw. "Did you have a nice Sunday?"

"Pardon? Oh, Sunday. It was okay."

A long silence became discomfiting. "You wanted to talk about something?" Kim finally reminded him.

Mitch took a swallow and lowered his beer bottle. "It's about us."

"I figured it was. What about us, Mitch?" Even though she was going to agree with everything he said, she couldn't see herself making it easy for him. He looked nervous and maybe he should. Without question, she'd been too pushy, but no man should make love to a woman the way Mitch had done with her if she wasn't important to him. Not when he knew she was falling hard and fast.

Mitch sat forward with the beer bottle braced in both hands between his spread knees, making an extremely masculine picture. Kim felt as though her heart was turning over in her chest. She loved him so much, more every day, and she was going to agree to never see him again. Her face felt frozen, stiff, from a phony expression of unruffled acceptance. This was tearing at her core, at that same portion of herself that defended the underdog and championed truth and fairness.

Mitch took another swallow of beer and looked at her. "If I don't say this right, don't get mad, okay?"

"I'm not going to get mad." She spoke in a monotone.

"I can't . . . do this anymore."

"Do what, Mitch." He didn't answer. "See me?"

He stood up. "I have to see you."

"What?" The word was sharp, but only because of Kim's surprise.

Mitch set down the beer bottle and began pacing. His agitation had him rubbing his mouth, then raking his hair. "I've been going in circles all week. Kim—"

The phone rang. Kim shot it a murderous look. Mitch had stopped in midstride. There was tumult in the air—his, hers.

They were on the verge of a breakthrough, and of all times for someone to call, this was the worst.

The ringing went on. "Go ahead and answer," Mitch told her.

Kim got up with a grim expression. She would cut the conversation short and get rid of whoever it was, impolitely if necessary.

She picked up the phone. "Hello?"

"Hello, Kim. This is Scot."

"Scot!" Kim smiled weakly and sent Mitch an apologetic glance. "How are you?"

"Just fine. How are things with you?"

"Actually... Scot, I have a guest. Could I call you back?"

"Sure, no problem. But this will only take a minute, Kim. I have to be in Seattle next week on a medical matter—something unexpected—and you mentioned getting together for an evening. I'm planning my itinerary and really need to know if Tuesday or Wednesday would be best for you."

"Uh... either is fine, Scot."

"Great. Let's set it for Wednesday. I'll call when I'm in the area."

"Do that, Scot."

"We'll have dinner and catch up, Kim."

"Wonderful." Kim was watching Mitch, who, oddly, seemed much quieter, much less agitated than he had been. "See you then, Scot. Bye."

Kim put down the phone. "That was an old friend."

"Was it?"

His expression was so strange, so withdrawn and guarded, that Kim's stomach dropped. "Scot Taylor and I grew up together, Mitch. Our parents were and still are very close friends. Scot is a pediatrician in California. A medical matter is bringing him to Seattle next week, and he wants us to spend an evening together. Actually, it was something I suggested at Dad's birthday party...."

"He was at Sarge's birthday party?"

Kim's mouth went dry. "It was a surprise to me. He had come home for the weekend and his folks brought him along. Mitch, Scot is no threat." There was a note of panic in her voice she couldn't abolish. Before Scot's call, Mitch had been very close to saying something important, probably closer to candor than he'd ever been with her. "He's a friend."

"Your kind of friend, Kim."

Her eyes widened. "Meaning?"

"A doctor? A lifelong friend of your parents? He's a perfect fit, isn't he?"

"A perfect fit for what? Mitch..." Kim moved across the room to address him at closer range. "You have the wrong impression. Scot Taylor is like a brother to me, and that's all he'll ever be."

Mitch's face was completely shut down. "I'm not jealous, so don't you get the wrong idea. But you live in a different world than I do. Your friends are people like Scot Taylor. He fits, Kim. I don't."

Tears suddenly blurred her vision. "How can you be so insensitive?"

"Insensitive! From where I'm standing, you're the one with the blinders." With a burst of passion, Mitch grabbed her hands and brought them up between them. His eyes were burning like two live coals. "Kim, open your eyes to reality. You and I don't have a chance."

"You thought we did when you came here tonight," she whispered tearily.

"That's not it. I had come up with some crazy notion that none of it mattered, and it does. You need a Scot Taylor. You deserve a Scot Taylor. Mitch Conover just doesn't cut it." He dropped her hands.

"That's absurd," she cried. "I don't want Scot or any other man. I want you!"

He turned his head to give her a cynical look. "You want me in the bedroom." He took a forward step. "I want you in the bedroom, too, more than I've ever wanted any woman. Right now, looking at you, being with you, having you is all I can think of. Is that good enough, Kim? Is a weekly roll in the hay enough for you? It's all I can give you."

When she moaned and tried to cover her face with her hands, he pulled them away and made her look at him. "Is it enough?"

"You weren't thinking like that when you got here," she accused, her voice trembling.

"Maybe I wasn't thinking at all."

Kim's anger exploded. "And maybe you were thinking more clearly than you have since we met! You said I deserve more than you. More of what, Mitch? A man with more money? More education? I happen to be struck dumb by a guy who works with his hands. Do you think I'm so crass as to denigrate your profession and go out looking for a man with a white-collar job? I don't give a damn what you do for a living! I don't give a damn that you work for my dad! I don't give a damn about anything but you!"

Taking a breath, Kim spoke more quietly. "You go ahead and keep on telling yourself you're not good enough, Mitch, but it's the biggest lie of the decade and someday you're going to realize it. For your sake, I hope that day of awakening won't come too late to bring you some happiness."

He was staring at her, still clasping her hands, his gaze roaming from feature to feature. "God help me if you're right," he mumbled.

"I am."

Her damp eyes grabbed and clutched at his soul. Her beautiful face conveyed misery, and it was his doing. "Kim . . . I'm sorry," he said hoarsely.

"Before you got here tonight, I vowed to agree to everything you said," she whispered. "I can't do it, Mitch. I can't agree to something that I know is more wrong than the worst mistake anyone ever made." Her eyes closed for a second. "Will you tell me the absolute truth about something?"

"I'll try. What is it?"

"Is there someone else?" She was looking into his eyes, probing for the truth.

His mouth twisted slightly. "There's no one else. Why would you think there was?"

"Because you couldn't get rid of me fast enough on Sunday."

"What I told you on Sunday was the truth. I'd promised to be somewhere at noon, and that's all there was to it."

He wasn't going to explain what that "somewhere" was, Kim realized. Maybe she could pry it out of him, but did she really want to try? Her eyes dropped to his hands gripping hers. She loved his hands. Big, powerful extensions of his very personality. Manly hands. She sighed sadly. Everything about Mitch was manly, even his voice, his gestures. Was that why she was so smitten, because he was the epitome of rugged masculinity?

"Would you like to finish your beer?" she asked huskily.

What he would like to do had nothing to do with food or drink. Mitch's lips thinned. Standing so close to Kim, even in anger, was affecting him. He'd felt her the second she'd opened the door. All week he'd struggled with standards and ethics, and she wasn't completely off base about his arrival mood: he'd come here with false hopes and ludicrous, childish ideas that nothing else mattered.

One kiss, he thought then. One kiss before he left. He brought her forward almost roughly, and gave her a hard, feverish kiss. By the way she gasped, he knew he'd surprised her. He broke the kiss and looked into her eyes.

"Is it enough?" he questioned.

"Is it enough for you?" she whispered.

"Right now it is."

He was grasping for moments, she realized, living in the present and avoiding the future. Didn't he know she loved him too much to say no?

"For me, too," she whispered, moving closer to his body, shivering when she was tightly molded to his chest and thighs.

Clasping her head to his chest, he sighed into the soft, silky strands of her hair. Where that "one kiss" idea had come from he couldn't begin to guess. One kiss would never satisfy either of them, a fact that had already been keeping him awake nights. He was getting in too deep with Kim, and he couldn't seem to slow the plunge, let alone halt it.

Still, there seemed to be a shell of dread around his emotions, too powerful to breach. Occasionally it slipped. Once in awhile it developed a crack, and his feelings seeped out and then raced around in his system wreaking havoc.

Holding Kim, he thought of the week in Olympia, and of the rumors he'd heard being discussed among the men. One of the head men in the company was retiring because of a medical problem. As a side effect, things were going to be happening within Armstrong Paving and Asphalt in the very near future—promotions, changes. Mitch's career hopes had become aroused again. His good reputation in the company was worthy of pride. Everything he'd gained thus far had been because of hard work, loyalty and dedication. And another promotion, should it come, would be for the same reasons. He couldn't risk his status, not even for... Kim.

He lowered his arms and moved back a step. Kim stared at him with startled eyes. "What's wrong now?" Her voice shook.

"The same old same old, Kim," he said quietly. "Do you grasp at all why I keep retreating?" She merely kept looking at him. "Have you mentioned me to your folks?"

"No, I have not," she said with the heat of sudden anger in her voice. "That's your biggest fear, isn't it? That Dad will learn of our relationship?"

"My fear isn't groundless."

"It's so ridiculously groundless, I marvel that the subject would even occur to an intelligent person," she snapped.

"Maybe I'm not so intelligent."

"Right now I believe it!" Clasping her arms around herself, Kim moved restlessly about the room.

"Scot Taylor is probably a lot more intelligent than me."

Kim whirled. "Don't bring Scot into this, Mitch. That's a damned cop-out."

Mitch's mouth tightened. "Fine. We'll leave him out of it, but you're kidding yourself if you think you and I are the only players in this little drama."

"We're the ones who count." Her voice had lost its sharp edge. She was losing the battle again, and frustration was edging out anger. If Scot hadn't called, if the telephone hadn't rung when it did, how far would Mitch have gone with his speech? Kim shivered from a sudden burst of anguish. What awful fate had decreed she fall in love with a reluctant man? A man with strange priorities and prejudices?

"Every person thinks he's the only one who counts, Kim, and that isn't even close to reality."

"To your reality, Mitch." She sounded weary, Kim realized, which was the simple truth. She was tired of waging a no-win battle, and if she did happen to win one day, would circumstances be any different? Without a major event of some sort—she couldn't imagine what it would take—Mitch wasn't going to change. Getting down to fundamentals, any change that Mitch underwent had to come from and through himself. Only he could adjust his priorities, his attitude. Certainly her turning into a nag and a shrew wasn't going to do it.

She brought her eyes to his and spoke without rancor. "I guess we each have to live with our own reality."

Her abruptly calmer tone and demeanor perplexed him. "Then you agree?"

Kim couldn't prevent a slight smirk. "If my agreeing makes you feel better, I guess that's what I'm doing. But tell me this. Exactly what am I agreeing to?"

Mitch cleared his throat. "To..." He rubbed his mouth. "I suppose we just agreed to staying away from each other."

"I suppose we did." How dull and lifeless she sounded. Sighing, Kim walked to a window and stared out. "It's almost dark," she said listlessly.

Mitch's eyes narrowed on her slender back, its bare upper portion, its inward curve to her waist. Was this it? The end of their battles, their opposition, their relationship? The heart and soul seemed to have gone out of him. He'd fought for division, for partition, and now that he had it, he felt like hell.

But it was the only sensible move he'd made in weeks. Since he'd received that invitation from Meridian Homes, to be exact.

He inched toward the door, moving as though his feet were burdened with heavy weights. Kim turned from the window. "Are you going now?"

"I might as well, don't you think?"

She stared. He wanted her to argue, to tell him not to leave! Understanding flooded her system. Mitch was as torn up as she was, and he might look like a pillar of strength, but he had as many insecurities as she did. Maybe more. Misery started somewhere in her midsection and radiated to even her scalp, her toes.

And then a strange calmness, coming out of nowhere, took over. She walked up to Mitch, aware of his eyes watching her progress. Standing in front of him, she spoke. "Let me show you my reality."

His only movement was a slight narrowing of his eyes. Kim stepped closer until there was no longer space between them. Laying her hands on his shoulders, she rose to tiptoe and pressed her mouth to his. His body stiffened for a second, then let go as he lifted his arms and locked them around her. His lips warmed and moved on hers. The kiss deepened and became passionate. Mitch's arms tightened around her. Kim's hands slid around his neck. She felt his tongue in her mouth and his heart going wild.

Then she tilted her head back to see his face. "That's my reality, Mitch," she whispered. "I guess what you do with it is up to you. Walk out, if you wish. Stay, if you wish. But accept the fact that whatever you do is your decision, not mine."

He was holding her, looking into her eyes, feeling her softness, her heat, inhaling her scent. "This isn't fair, Kim."

"Please don't mention fairness. Nothing has been fair since we met." Kim extracted herself from his arms, and he stood there with a bereft expression that wrung out her heart. "It's up to you, Mitch."

His internal battle showed on his face. Stay or go. It had always been his decision, hadn't it? Why did it seem so much more acute now? So painfully defined? He grasped at parallels, realizing that he was at a particularly crucial crossroads. For the first time in their troubled relationship, Kim would accept a negative decision from him. He could see on her face that if he walked out now, she wouldn't manipulate another meeting.

He drew in a long, tortured breath. He couldn't keep doing this. It was Kim or his job; he couldn't have both.

Slowly he turned and walked to the door. "Goodbye, Kim."

Her eyes filled. "Goodbye."

His final look was weighted with anguish. She saw and recognized it, and she stood there and watched him open the door. It closed behind him.

"Oh, Mitch," she whispered brokenly, so crushed she wondered if she would ever recover.

Eight

"Kim, honey, I'm throwing a party to mark Morey Holman's retirement, and I'd like you to be there."

Kim sat down at the desk in her studio. Sarge rarely called during working hours, and when he did, it was usually for something important. "Morey's retiring? How come, Dad?"

"Doctor's orders."

"Morey is ill?" Kim didn't see much of the company's executives these days, but she knew them all and hated hearing that one of them wasn't well.

"Afraid so, Kim. It's his heart. Don't worry. He'll be fine for a long time with the proper care, but he can't continue working. Anyway, this all came up pretty sudden. Just heard about it myself last week. I can't let Morey leave without a little send-off, Kim. Everyone in the company will be there and I'd like you to show up. Can you make it?"

"Yes, of course. When is it, Dad?" Everyone in the company was going to be there? Mitch, too? Kim's pulse began racing. Since Friday evening she had been going through hell. One minute she told herself to put her energy into forgetting Mitch, and the next she teared up and felt disconnected with life itself.

"Wednesday night at the Regency," Sarge said. "Seven o'clock."

The Regency was Sarge's favorite restaurant, a rather elegant establishment that provided private dining rooms for groups, large and small.

"Wednesday night?" Kim frowned at this unexpected curve. "Dad, Scot Taylor is going to be in the area, and I promised to have dinner with him on Wednesday."

"That's no problem, honey. Bring Scot along. I'll add his name to the guest list."

A scenario unfolded in Kim's mind, her walking in on Scot's arm, Mitch seeing her, her waving casually, Mitch's expression getting grim. Didn't he deserve something like that? He'd said the two of them weren't the only players in this little drama, and all of the players would be present— her parents, herself and Mitch. Maybe this was what she'd been hoping for, a chance to expose her and Mitch's relationship. And it wasn't her doing. It would be a meeting she hadn't caused, and in no way could Mitch get annoyed about it. If he should happen to be bothered enough to do some checking, he would merely learn that Sarge often included her in company functions.

"I'll be there, Dad," she said with a smile more cheerful than she had mustered in days.

"I'm sure Scot won't mind," Sarge said.

Kim was of a frame of mind to agree. "No reason he should. We were just going to do some catching up, which I'm sure we can manage at some point of the evening."

"Wear something pretty, honey. It's not going to be formal, but I've told everyone to dress up. Morey deserves a fine showing."

"I will." Not just pretty, but stunning, she promised herself. Knocking Mitch's socks off had already become of the utmost necessity in her mind.

And so Kim went shopping. In between sessions in her studio and appointments with clients, she haunted her favorite stores. To her delight she found the perfect dress, a high-fashion black chiffon-and-sequin creation that reeked of glamour and sophistication. Black, very high-heeled pumps, black hose, black onyx and rhinestone earrings and a tiny black evening bag completed the ensemble.

Scot called on Tuesday. "I'm in Seattle, Kim."

"Great. Are you staying with your folks?"

"I wouldn't dare stay anywhere else," Scot replied with a laugh. "Tomorrow I'll be in conference all day, but I should be free by four. What time should I pick you up?"

Kim drew a breath. "Scot, something came up. Dad is giving a party for an unexpected retiree in the company. He wants me to attend, and, you guessed it, it's scheduled for tomorrow night. I told him about our date and he said to bring you along. What do you say? I really can't get out of going, but I want to see you, too. Would you mind going to the affair?"

"I suppose it would be all right."

He wasn't thrilled, Kim could tell, feeling a little guilty about imposing on Scot's good nature. "You're a lifesaver, Scot, thanks. It starts at seven and shouldn't last more than a few hours. We can do our catching up after it's over."

Scot agreed, and they hung up after a few minutes of small talk, both of them obviously saving the important stuff for tomorrow night. The idea of putting Scot and Mitch in the same room did create a bit of uneasiness, but there wasn't a reason in the world for Mitch to resent her seeing an old friend. Not that she had any guarantee he would resent anything. He might take one look and be glad he'd broken off with her.

On the other hand—and this thought was much more comforting—he might take one look at her in her fabulous dress, not even see Scot, and realize how foolish his attitude was.

Kim went home early on Wednesday, arriving at the condo around four. Admittedly her nerves were on edge, but, by the same token, there was so much excitement in her system, she was practically choking on it.

It was only after she had bathed, fixed her hair and makeup, dressed in filmy lingerie and slid into the luscious dress that what she was doing really struck home. Her mirror reflected glamour. The overall effect of the dress and her own efforts were almost shocking. She looked like someone else!

"Oh, Lord," she whispered, shaken by what she saw in the mirror. Unquestionably she looked terrific, but was this the best image to project tonight? What was Mitch's mood now? Had he successfully put her out of his mind? What would she gain by blasting him with a glamour-girl image, which was so far from the truth to be laughable.

She had nearly made an awful mistake. Carefully stepping out of the gorgeous dress, Kim returned it to its protective cover and hung it in the closet. Someday she would wear it, hopefully for Mitch, but not tonight. Not when she was going to walk in with another man, good friend or not. Everything about the evening suddenly felt wrong, especially arriving with Scot.

But that was something she couldn't change. Sighing disconsolately, Kim chose another dress, probably the one she would have worn if she hadn't gotten so carried away with that fantasy about knocking off Mitch's socks. It was red with a swirly skirt and a fitted bodice, a pretty dress. Kim exchanged the black hose for a neutral shade, and found the red pumps that matched the dress.

Her reflection was much more satisfying. She looked good without the shock value. Normal. Herself.

Scot rang the bell at six-thirty. Kim opened the door with a smile. "Hi."

"Hi, yourself. Give us a hug." He gathered her up for a friendly hug, then looked at her. "Everything okay?"

"No, and it shows, doesn't it?"

"What's wrong?"

"Come on in. We've got a few minutes before we have to leave." Kim led him into the living room. They sat down.

Scot looked fantastic in a deep-blue suit and tie with a white shirt. His good looks worried Kim. "Tonight could turn out to be the biggest fiasco of my life," she said gloomily.

"How come?"

"Mitch is going to be there."

"Mitch is the guy you mentioned at Sarge's birthday party?"

"The same."

"And?" Scot looked somewhat perplexed.

An honest explanation was on the tip of Kim's tongue. *Walking in with you isn't exactly going to better my case with Mitch, Scot.* But Scot's feelings rated some consideration, too, not just hers and Mitch's. She'd been the one to suggest a get-together; Scot had been kind enough to include an evening with her in his schedule; and, hinting now that he might be in the way tonight would be a deplorable thing to do.

"Dad and Mother are still in the dark about our relationship," Kim said quietly, adding after a moment, "Such as it is."

"It's not going well?"

"Right now it's not going at all," Kim admitted. "We agreed not to see each other anymore." She could tell that the conversation was only causing Scot perplexity. Unless she explained in detail, he couldn't begin to grasp the situation.

She changed the subject. "How are you and Candace doing?"

Scot's expression cleared. "We're going to be married, Kim. I told my folks, and they're planning a trip to California in August to meet Candace."

Kim offered a genuine smile. "That's great, Scot. I'm very happy for you. Congratulations."

"You'll be getting an invitation to the wedding."

"Which will take place when?"

"In December."

"Wonderful," Kim murmured, envisioning a beautiful Christmas wedding. She smiled wistfully. "I just realized something, Scot. You're the last of my friends who've never been married. A few of them are divorced, but everyone from the old crowd has been married at least once. After December, I'll be the only holdout.''

"Hey, it'll happen," Scot said, sounding emphatic. "You'll fall in love and tie the knot, same as everyone else.''

"Maybe, maybe not." Kim got to her feet. "I'll get my bag. It's time to go.''

The Regency was lighted up like a starry sky, and its parking lot was packed. "We'll valet park," Scot said.

"Fine." Kim pulled down the visor for a final look in the mirror. Along with feeling light-headed, her stomach was jumping around and fluttering as though inhabited by butterflies. No matter how exotic or delicious the food served tonight, she wouldn't be able to eat a bite. In fact, if she became any more jittery, she was apt to do something bizarre, like fainting.

No, she definitely was not going to faint. But why did she never do anything completely right where Mitch was concerned? Whatever happened to the calm, poised and usually composed woman she'd been before meeting Mitch Conover? Where was that Kimberly Armstrong hiding these days?

"Ready?" Scot asked her as the valet attendant opened his door.

"Ready," Kim echoed, which was probably the truth. She was, after all, as ready to walk into the Regency as she could ever be. Which wasn't saying much. Recent choices bobbed around in her brain. She should have told her dad that she had other plans when he called to invite her to tonight's affair, without explaining what those plans were. Her own big mouth got her into this. Naturally, Sarge would tell her to bring Scot along.

Kim's door was swung open by a second attendant. "Evening, ma'am.''

"Hi." She took the young man's hand while barely registering that he was a young man. Inside, in one of the Regency's elegant private party rooms, was Mitch. Unsuspecting, no doubt, unaware that she'd been invited and due for one enormous surprise. She could have arranged things differently, met Scot afterwards, for instance. For that matter, she could have pretended to come down with the flu and skipped the entire evening!

And, yet, wasn't something like this what she'd been hoping for? An opportunity to bring Mitch and her folks together in a social environment? Not for the Armstrongs' benefit, but for Mitch's. If he once realized that Sarge and Sara couldn't care less whom their daughter was dating, wouldn't he settle down and lose his previous objections?

"It's being held in the Crystal Room," Kim murmured as they went through the Regency's automatic front doors and she spotted a sign that read, Armstrong Paving and Asphalt, Crystal Room. "Down that hall, Scot."

He walked with his hand at the small of her back, which she would hardly have noticed at any other time. Tonight the gesture seemed more possessive than protective, which wasn't even close to the truth. But she couldn't just shake off Scot's hand, not when she knew he meant nothing by it, and she certainly wasn't going to tell him that Mitch might be jealous of an old friend's politeness. Besides, Mitch himself had stated very clearly that he wasn't jealous of Scot. Her misgivings were really a result of her own insecurities, she thought uneasily, and not to be passed on to Scot or anyone else.

Music reached their ears. People were coming and going. Kim said hello to several in passing, and then, before them, were the large double doors opening onto the Crystal Room. Kim drew in a deep breath. "Here we are."

They stood within the wide doorway and looked into the room. "Good turnout," Scot commented.

The crowd swam before Kim's eyes—men in suits and ties, women in colorful dresses. Her gaze settled down and skimmed the groups, and almost immediately she saw Mitch. He was talking with two men and a woman, standing casually with a glass in one hand and his other hand in the pocket of his pants.

"That's him," she whispered. Her heart was doing flips in her chest, matching the instability of her stomach.

Apparently Scot hadn't heard. "There's Sarge. He's coming over."

Sarge walked up grinning. "Why are you two standing in the doorway? Hello, Scot." They shook hands. Sarge turned to his daughter and gave her a hug. "You look great, honey."

"So do you, Dad. Where's Mother?"

Sarge looked around. "She's . . . There she is, talking to the Holmans. Go on over and say hello to Morey and Betty." Kim and Scot started away. "And get yourself a drink, Scot. The bar's right across the room."

Kim led the way as they wound through the crowd. "Do you want a drink, Scot?"

"Not right now, thanks."

They walked up to Sara and the Holmans. "Hello, Mother," Kim said, and then smiled at the others. "Hello."

Morey and Betty both said hello. Morey took Kim's hand. "How are you, honey? Haven't seen you in a long time."

"I'm fine, Morey." Kim tried to look cheerful. "I understand this party is for you. You're finally quitting the rat race, I hear."

Morey gave a small laugh. "Well, I'd rather stay right in the middle of it, Kim, but you know how it goes."

"Morey, I don't think you and Betty know Scot Taylor."

While they were shaking hands and acknowledging the introduction, Kim spoke to her mother. "Nice gathering, Mother. I know Dad picked the Regency, but I'll bet you took care of the details."

Sara laughed. "Guilty. We're having a sit-down dinner in about a half hour and there'll be dancing after the speeches. I'm glad you could make it, Kim. Your father always likes to have you at these functions."

"Yes, I know." Kim eyed the four-piece band across the room, which was presently playing soft background music.

Dancing hadn't occurred to her. Ordinarily these affairs wound down after a few hours. Apparently Sarge had wanted to go all out for Morey's retirement party.

Something else hadn't occurred to her, she realized. The married men and women in the company had brought their spouses; the single people had probably brought dates. Maybe Mitch wasn't here alone. The thought weakened Kim's knees. Why was she constantly getting surprised with Mitch? Had her ability to think clearly vanished entirely when she fell in love?

Kim's mouth was suddenly dry. "I'm going to the bar," she murmured to Scot, and to the others she smiled and said, "I'll see you later."

At the bar she ordered her usual soda water with a twist of lime, and Scot ordered a cola drink. Kim sipped and then, unerringly, she found Mitch in the crowd again. Obviously he hadn't yet seen her. People were milling, mingling, moving around to chat and laugh with each other. Everyone seemed to know everyone else, and also seemed to be enjoying themselves.

"Would you like to sit down?" Scot asked.

"Yes, but there are people I should say hello to." She smiled apologetically. "I'm sorry I got you into this."

He smiled indulgently. "I'll live. And don't worry about me, Kim. Feel free to wander and do your duty. I'll find someone to talk to, or a place to sit. I'll be fine." Scot turned and scanned the room. "Incidentally, which guy is yours?"

Kim nearly choked. Not because of Scot's question, but because of the immediate reply she felt deep inside of herself: *Don't I wish!*

"He's standing almost in the center of the room, Scot, talking to some people. See the woman wearing a bright yellow dress? He's the man on the right."

Scot picked him out. "Hmm. Nice-looking guy."

"Yes, he is." Nice-looking was a gross understatement. Mitch stood out, taller than most, crisper, more handsome than any, dark and stunning in a wonderfully cut suit and shiny black shoes. What made him think he didn't fit in?

His clothes tonight were proof that he knew how to dress for
an occasion, and it was obvious that his co-workers liked
him.

For a moment Kim suffered an almost intolerable urge to
march up to the podium and announce over the microphone that she was in love with Mitch Conover and didn't
care who knew it!

Of course, it was only silly fantasy. That sort of public
display would destroy any slim chance she and Mitch still
had. Kim knew she was grasping at straws by hanging onto
a thread of hope at all. He'd made his choice last weekend
and pressured her into an agreement.

But he knew she wasn't happy about it, and given her past
boldness, maybe an announcement from the podium
wouldn't even surprise him.

Kim sighed and sipped from her glass. Several people had
waved, and she really must speak to them. "I'll wander a
bit, Scot. Are you sure you don't mind?"

"Not at all. Go to it, kid."

His grin was reassuring. "See you later."

Kim took a few hesitant steps, then veered in a direction
that would skirt Mitch's position in the room. Almost instantly she ran into a couple she knew.

Mitch shifted his weight from one foot to another and
looked around. Nodding at one of his crew members and his
wife some distance away, his gaze moved through the mass.
He caught sight of Sarge and a few seconds later, of Sara.
They were great hosts. At one end of the room, tables were
set for dinner. The bar was open and the live music was entertaining. The Armstrongs knew how to throw a party;
everyone was enjoying the event, himself included, and he'd
never been particularly fond of parties.

A woman in a red dress caught his eye. Her back was all
he could see of her, but her long dark hair struck a familiar
chord. His eyes narrowed as a buzzing began in his system.
Kim . . . she looked like Kim.

But did she attend company functions? Why would she?
On the other hand, why wouldn't she? He racked his brain

to recall last year's Christmas party. Had she been there? Would he have missed her, if she had?

The woman laughed about something and turned her head. Mitch's heart took a leap. Kim! Kim was here, looking radiant in a red dress, laughing with friends.

Mitch looked down at his glass and saw that it contained nothing but bits of melting ice. "I'm going to get a refill," he told his companions, and walked off to the bar.

"Another ginger ale," he said to the bartender. He wasn't drinking beer or anything harder on purpose, as he wanted to remain levelheaded at a function like this one. Now, standing at the bar, he wondered if a stiff belt wouldn't alleviate the sharp ache in his gut. The Armstrongs, all three, darted around in his mind. If he believed Kim, Sara and Sarge knew nothing of their relationship. The facade he and Kim were wearing felt like a sham, like something shoddy and underhanded.

Damn, if he'd only had some warning. If he'd known beforehand that Kim was going to be here, he would have been better prepared to act nonplussed.

The bartender delivered his drink. "Thanks." Mitch picked up the glass and noticed a tall man with blond hair standing nearby and looking at him. He nodded. The man nodded.

What the hell. It was a party, and there were probably people here he should meet. Mitch walked over to the stranger and offered his hand. "Mitch Conover."

Scot shook his hand. "Scot Taylor."

Mitch felt himself blanch. Taylor was here with Kim! This was the date he'd heard discussed on the phone in Kim's condo last Friday night!

"Uh...nice meeting you," he managed to mumble.

"Good meeting you," Scot returned with a friendly smile.

Mitch didn't know where to put himself, nor what to say. "I..." His befuddled mind landed on a safe topic. "I didn't know Kim was going to be here tonight."

"Sarge insisted she come. I think he likes her to be involved with the company wherever possible."

"Understandable."

"Yes, it is," Scot agreed. "If she were a man, she'd probably be working for the company."

"She could still work there. Other women do."

"That's not the point, Mitch. Kim's interest is interior design, not business. I remember when Sarge and Sara bought their house. Kim was around eleven, twelve, at the time, and she became so fascinated with decorating, she didn't want to do anything but follow Sara around to the stores and shops. Believe it or not, before Sara was finished with that house, she was asking for Kim's opinion on colors and which chair would look best in which corner. She has a natural talent for the art, Mitch, and in my opinion, decorating a building to conform with a client's taste and style is definitely an art form."

How well Scot Taylor knew Kim. How little Mitch Conover knew about Kim. There was something else gnawing a hole in his gut. Scot was no slouch. He was good-looking and intelligent, a guy too levelheaded not to see Kim Armstrong's value. Maybe Kim thought of Scot as an old friend, but Mitch would bet anything that Dr. Scot Taylor had other ideas about her.

Whatever, Taylor was here and with Kim. Her date for the evening. Probably her date every time he came to Seattle. As Mitch had told Kim, Dr. Taylor fit in with the Armstrongs; Mitch Conover did not.

"What do you do in the company?" Scot inquired.

Across the room, Kim happened to glance toward the bar. Her heart nearly stopped beating. Mitch and Scot! How had they met so quickly? What were they discussing? Would they talk about her?

"Excuse me," she murmured, deserting the couple with whom she'd been talking. Then she wove her way through the groups, speaking to some, though absentmindedly, intent on reaching the two men near the bar.

"Kim!"

She stopped. Sarge was wending his way over to her. "Having a good time, honey?"

"It's a nice party, Dad." Nervously she glanced at Scot and Mitch.

"There's something I'd like you to know, honey. After dinner I'm going to give a little speech about Morey's retirement, and I'm going to say a few words about my own retirement. I didn't want it to take you by surprise."

Every other thought fled Kim's mind. "Your retirement! Dad, are you ill, too?"

"No," Sarge said quickly. "I'm fit as a fiddle, Kim, so banish that idea once and for all. But your mother and I've been doing some serious talking since we learned of Morey's disability. We're not getting any younger, and if we're ever going to do that traveling we've always talked about, we'd best get to it."

Kim visibly relaxed. "Great. I couldn't agree more. Thanks for warning me. If you'd made that announcement from the podium, I might have keeled over with a heart attack."

Sarge chuckled. "You're made of stronger stuff than that, honey. Anyway, you have a good time. We'll talk again later."

Kim laid a restraining hand on his arm. "Dad, with Morey retiring and now yourself, who will run the company?"

Sarge patted her hand. "We've got some terrific young men in the ranks, Kim. There are going to be some mighty big changes and promotions in the very near future."

Instead of feeling grateful that Sarge wasn't worried about his replacement, or Morey's, Kim's heart sank. "That's good, Dad," she murmured. "See you later." She stared after Sarge as he walked off. Mitch would be more focused on his career than ever. Plus, if he didn't attain every upward step completely on his own, he would forever suffer doubts about whether he had truly earned them.

Heaving a sigh, Kim again pointed herself in the direction of the bar.

Nine

Mitch saw her coming. His spine stiffened as he forced an unconcerned expression.

Kim walked up. "Hello, Mitch." His immobile features didn't fool her. She didn't have to see his tension when she sensed it so well.

"Hello, Kim."

Scot discreetly backed away and neither Kim nor Mitch noticed.

"I'm sure my being here surprised you," she murmured, hoping to put them both at ease.

"Did my being here surprise you?"

"Of course not. You're a part of the company." Kim added after a beat, "Dad wanted me to be here."

"You don't have to explain or apologize."

"I'm not apologizing!" Looking away from his deep blue eyes, Kim bit her lip. Did he really think she had apologized for attending her own father's party? "There will be other events like this, so you may as well get used to my involvement."

"You weren't at the Christmas party," he said, almost accusingly.

"No, I wasn't. I volunteer for several charities, and one of them held their own Christmas party on the same evening."

"I've attended other company functions, and I don't remember you being there."

Kim frowned. Had she really missed every company affair since Mitch's employment? Sarge had invited her, she knew.

"I can't explain my absence from every event," she confessed. "But Dad always asks me to attend." It was true. Sarge never failed to include her.

She thought of what Sarge had said about retirement and felt a pang. There must have been times when he regretted not having a son, and maybe even moments when he rued his daughter having absolutely no affinity with the business world. He had never hinted to her that he might wish she had been born a boy, or that she had shown an interest in the company he had spent his life building, but how could she doubt that those thoughts had crossed his mind?

An announcement from the podium interrupted Kim's uneasy reflection of a subject that had never before occurred to her. "People...friends...guests...please find your seats at the tables. Dinner is going to be served."

The crowd began shuffling toward the tables. Kim's gaze connected with Mitch's. Now she would find out for sure if he had brought a date. "Guess it's time to eat," she said with studied casualness.

He kept looking at her. "Guess it is."

There was something so intense in his eyes, messages unsaid and not quite readable. She was sending messages, too, but did he grasp at all how much seeing him and acting as though they were mere acquaintances hurt? Her facade wilted. "Oh, Mitch," she whispered. "Is this really the way it's going to be?"

He tore his gaze from hers to frown at the crowd. Among the company men and women was an air of excitement. No one was applauding Morey's early retirement, but it meant a shake-up within the company structure that couldn't be ignored. Mitch could feel the high energy of those with ambition and hope, himself included. When things started happening, which he felt would come very soon, he had to be ready.

His choices and decisions since meeting Kim gnawed at him. Within the groups beginning to sit down were Sarge and Sara, presently joining Morey and Betty Holman and two other couples at the head table. The Armstrongs had no inkling of the true nature of their daughter's and Mitch Conover's relationship, which bore the distinct taint of deceit—his deceit. If he was going to continue working for Sarge, the deception had to stop.

As many decisions as he had made and attempted to make during the last month, tonight's—looking Kim in the eye and telling her that, yes, this was the way it was going to be—hurt more than the others. Maybe because of Scot Taylor, who was a hell of a nice guy, good-looking, a friend of the Armstrong family and a doctor to boot. It wasn't that he was jealous of Scot, it was that the young medic was so perfect for Kim. So damned perfect.

"Sorry," he said quietly, tonelessly.

Something suddenly rebelled in Kim. This had gone far enough—her mewling and all but begging, Mitch occasionally succumbing then denying. Yes, it had definitely gone on long enough.

Her chin came up in a prideful gesture. "See you around, Mitch." She walked off to where Scot was standing and took his arm. "Let's join the others."

Broodingly Mitch stared after her. She was vibrant in that red dress, a brightness in the large room that outshone everyone and everything else. No two people should have to deal with his and Kim's situation. If he worked for someone else, there wouldn't *be* a situation. Unconnected with Sarge's company, he could give Scot Taylor a run for his money. Deep down Mitch knew he would win.

His frown deepened. Maybe his priorities were completely screwed up. Maybe he should be concentrating on a career change. Looking for another job. By digging in his heels and stubbornly staying put, he was losing the only woman he had ever loved.

The thought was staggering. He was in love with Kim Armstrong. Not infatuated, not merely stricken by lust, but in love. How had it happened? *When* had it happened? At their first meeting? Their second?

Mitch set his glass on the bar. Nearly everyone was seated. Grimly, he crossed the room to find his table. Place cards denoted the seating arrangement. His table, he realized, was between Kim's and the podium and set at an angle so that she would have a clear view of him and he wouldn't be able to see her without turning around.

From her seat Kim watched Mitch find his. Resentment broiled. The glaring bottom line was too harsh to ignore: his job was more important than she was. Maybe his attitude against mingling his work and personal life wasn't completely irrational, but he was actively choosing his job over her. And she would be a fool to forget it again.

She drew in a long, disconsolate breath. From here on in she would forget nothing, not how much of a fool she had already made of herself, not Mitch's pigheadedness and certainly not her brand-new vow to stay totally out of his life. He could concentrate solely on his precious career from here on in.

Or... he could stuff it up his nose.

The dinner courses were served with the Regency's usual flair and efficiency. As the dessert plates were being picked up and coffee cups refilled, Sarge went to the podium.

"Folks... let me have your attention."

The buzz of conversation faded. Wishing wholeheartedly that she had eluded this event, Kim sent Scot an apologetic glance. Burdening him with this sort of evening had been thoughtless and inconsiderate.

Sarge's voice carried over the microphone. "You all know why we're here tonight. But first, let me thank everyone for making it a hundred-percent turnout." A burst of applause broke out.

All Kim could see of Mitch was the back of his head. Her gaze alternated from red-hot to freezing cold. What was wrong with the man? Didn't he know the high cost of his peculiar attitude? Obviously his thought processes occurred in different patterns and priorities than hers—possibly different than anyone's she'd ever known—but did that give him a license to inflict so much pain?

Sarge's speech regarding Morey's years with the company barely registered while Kim pondered her own problems. Blaming Mitch for her pain wasn't being totally upfront and honest. Right from the onset of their disoriented and disorganized relationship, she'd known how risky her persistence was. She had gambled with her heart...and lost.

The audience was silent and listening to Sarge with admirable interest. "So," he said, "while the company, myself in particular, will miss Morey, we will bear up and go on from here. Morey..." Sarge looked over to his longtime employee. "I have a little departure gift, if you would come up here and receive it."

Grinning self-consciously, Morey pushed back his chair. Sarge said into the microphone, while Morey was striding to the podium, "I'd like to add that Morey isn't the only company man going into retirement. My own retirement is imminent."

An audible gasp rolled through the crowd. Chuckling, Sarge held up his hand. "Not this very minute, gang, so relax. You can expect an announcement within the next month or so."

Mitch felt frozen to his chair. Sarge was going to retire? The changes in the company were going to be even more drastic than he'd thought. His pulse suddenly took off. If ever a man was suddenly besieged with opportunity, it was him. Leaving the company at this auspicious time would be complete folly, the height of shortsightedness.

Cautiously he moved his head, hoping to catch a glimpse of Kim without blatantly turning around. All he could see was the red of her dress, and that was on the very edge of his peripheral vision. Facing front again, he rubbed his mouth with a taut hand. More than ever it was Kim or his job, the success he'd always dreamed of attaining or the woman he loved.

Morey opened a small box. "It's a Rolex!" Everyone laughed at his pleased surprise, but Kim caught the emotion between the two men at the podium. "Sarge...thanks." They shook hands.

"Morey, old friend, you deserve the best." Sarge slapped him on the back. They hugged, and Kim would have bet anything that her dad's eyes contained tears. Her own throat felt constricted from emotion. The whole evening had been emotional, in one way or another.

Sarge spoke again. "That's it for the formalities, folks. Enjoy yourselves now. The band will play your favorite songs for dancing, and the bar will remain open for another two hours. Remember our rule, though. The designated driver doesn't drink at company parties."

The audience rose and applauded with passionate approval. Some of the men whistled raucously. People began drifting away from the tables. The band started playing a spirited tune.

Scot turned to Kim. "It went well, don't you think?"

"Very well." Kim was trying to see Mitch through the crowd and failing. Pushing her chair back, she stood up. "Let's say good-night to Mother and Dad and leave."

Frowning slightly, Scot got to his feet. "Are you sure?"

"Very." There was a lifelessness in Kim's voice, but hanging around hoping for another chance to talk to Mitch would be utterly insane. "There's Mother," she murmured, catching sight of Sara among a group.

They started walking in Sara's direction when Kim stopped dead. Standing to one side were Sarge and Mitch, talking like two old pals. The gorge rose in Kim's throat. Never would she accuse Mitch of buttering up the boss; he simply wasn't the type to butter up anyone, and who knew better than she that his only interest in Sarge Armstrong was work-related?

But the two of them talking so earnestly rubbed her wrong. Instead of continuing on to her mother, she veered to approach her father.

"Dad?"

Sarge turned. He was smiling. "Hi, honey. Having a good time?"

"Scot and I are leaving, Dad." Kim leaned forward to kiss Sarge's cheek. "We just wanted to say good-night." Over her father's shoulder she gave Mitch an icy look, and his face darkened by three shades.

"Do you have to rush off?" Sarge questioned.

"Afraid so." Kim stepped back while Scot and Sarge shook hands. Deliberately, she avoided looking at Mitch again. He didn't want her, didn't need her and probably hoped never to see her again. The ache in her body was a raw wound and apt to remain so for the rest of her days. She vowed—swore—to never fall in love again, even if it meant living out her life completely alone.

Then Mitch had the gall to say, quietly, "Good night, Kim." Gritting her teeth until they hurt, she whirled and walked away.

"Good night, honey," Sarge called.

Scot followed, all but running to catch up. "Hey, what's your hurry?"

Kim slowed her furious steps. "I want to get out of here."

"Obviously," Scot said dryly. "Sara's in the other direction, in case you forgot."

They were nearly to the door. "I'll call Mother in the morning."

The long hall to the Regency's front foyer was quickly eaten up by Kim's haste. Stepping outside, she inhaled deeply, finding the fresh night air mentally reviving, however weak and trembling were her legs. "I'm sorry, Scot, truly sorry," she said. "I never should have forced tonight on you."

"Forget it, Kim. Let's go somewhere and have a cup of coffee."

It was midnight when Scot brought her home. The only sin she hadn't committed with her old friend was to actually cry on his shoulder. Occupying a booth in an all-night diner, she had unloaded every worry, every emotion, every joy and pain that she had felt since meeting Mitch. Scot had listened with very little comment, apparently recognizing her need to just let go and talk.

But before getting out of the car, Kim said, "You haven't said much about my sad story, Scot. Tell me what you think, please."

"Kim, I'm not a woman. Men think differently about their careers."

"That's simply not true," she ardently rebutted. "Women are as passionate about their careers as men are, but I think Mitch's passion has evolved into obsession. Please don't turn chauvinistic on me, Scot. You're the only person I've confided in, and I would appreciate your honest opinion."

"Well . . . all right. I hardly know Mitch, but the few minutes we talked makes me think he's a stand-up guy. Kim, from everything you've told me, he merely wants to get ahead on his own. Maybe he's carrying it too far, but can you really fault the guy for trying to keep his personal affairs separate from his job?"

"I'm not just a personal affair!" she cried. Then she crumpled. "That's not true. I don't know what I am to him, and that's what hurts." After a moment, she slid across the seat to kiss Scot's cheek. "If you ever have another free evening in Seattle and call me, I promise not to be such an awful drag."

Scot put his arms around her. "Don't be so hard on yourself, Kim. You're only human, like the rest of us, and I don't know one single person who actually got to choose who he or she fell in love with."

They sat in silence. Being held was comforting for Kim. Until Scot's last remark really sunk in, that is. She pulled away. "You do know one person who chose his own fate, Scot. Mitch is doing exactly that." She slid across the seat to the door. "Don't get out. It's only a few steps to my condo and the area is well-lighted." Somehow she managed a smile. "Thanks, Scot. It was great seeing you."

"It was great seeing you. Try to be happy, Kim."

She opened the door. "I will. Good night."

Kim trudged the short distance to her condo, unlocked the door and turned to wave at Scot. She heard his car driving away after she was inside.

Not fifty feet from where Scot had parked was Mitch's pickup, with him sitting behind the wheel. An hour ago he had rang Kim's doorbell. Why he hadn't immediately left when her absence became apparent was a question without an answer. But there he was, an eyewitness to the touching good-night scene between Kim and Scot. Oh, yes, he'd seen plenty. The numerous pole lights in the compound had illuminated the lengthy embrace in the front seat of Taylor's car, and Mitch had painfully endured it while wondering if Kim was going to invite her date in.

It appeared that she hadn't. Or maybe Scot had had to leave for some reason. Whatever, Kim was home now and alone.

Mitch's stomach was roiling with tension. Why was he here? Why had he come at all, let alone waited for an hour? Apparently Kim hadn't noticed his truck, which was in plain sight and hard to miss. Mitch's mouth thinned. She'd been occupied with Scot, probably hanging on his every word.

At the picture his own brain had devised, Mitch disgustedly shook his head. Kim hanging on *anyone's* every word just didn't compute. Who knew better than him that she was a woman with a strong mind that wasn't easily influenced by other people's ideas and opinions?

Mitch stared at the lighted windows in Kim's condo. Torn by emotions that persisted in pestering him, he'd driven here from the Regency instead of going home. He hated the tension between him and Kim, and would like to smooth things out. Not in the name of romance, but because neither of them should have to walk on eggshells around the other. And Kim was right: events of tonight's nature were bound to bring them together time and again. Unless he left the company.

The freedom to pursue Kim openly, actively, looked so appealing, and he sat there and thought about it. It would feel great to call her, or to simply knock on her door and announce that there was no longer any reason for reluctance. Their relationship could advance as fast as they wanted. They could see each other whenever and wherever. He could meet her parents with an honest face, holding Kim's hand, if he felt like it, showing the Armstrongs how much he cared for their daughter.

They... could get married.

Mitch groaned aloud. He was at a crucial crossroads. One direction led to the woman he wanted to the point of agony; the other led to the financial success he had always dreamed of attaining. He was so torn by his choices he felt queasy.

With his mouth set grimly, he reached for the ignition key. But something stopped him from turning it, and he sat without moving, his forefinger and thumb clasping the key. He was leaning toward the path leading to Kim, he realized, his eyes narrowing in introspection, leaning harder by the second, getting desperate for her warmth, her softness, her response. Losing her was suddenly the worst fate that could befall him. How could any job compare, even one with a virtually unlimited future?

He had to see her. Her lights were still on, so she hadn't immediately gone to bed. Pocketing the key, Mitch deserted the pickup, strode to Kim's door and pushed the doorbell button.

Kim nearly jumped out of her skin. Too keyed up for sleep, she had exchanged her dress for a comfortable cotton wrapper with a sash at the waist, and she'd been pacing, going from room to room while trying to still the turmoil in her system, telling herself one minute that Mitch wasn't the only fish in the sea, and the next, renewing her vow to live out her life without any man.

During her three-year residency at this condo, no one had ever rung the doorbell after midnight. It had an ominous sound, and she nervously crept to the door to peer out the peephole. Seeing Mitch felt like a blow, and her mood instantly switched from nervous to furious. She yanked open the door.

"Hi," he said, his gaze flicking down her pale pink robe and back up to her face.

"What do you want?" It wasn't said politely.

He hadn't expected anger, but there was no denying the snapping furor in Kim's eyes. "Are you too mad at me to talk?"

"You want to talk. Gee, should I be thrilled?"

Her sarcasm made Mitch wince. "May I come in?"

A fast and fierce battle went on behind Kim's eyes. She could slam the door in his face, which was only what he deserved, or she could let him come in and unload her pent-up wrath, which was something else he deserved. In any case, she couldn't keep him standing on her stoop, not when sound carried so well at night and her neighbors' units were all dark.

She moved back from the door, a seethingly silent invitation to enter. Mitch took a breath and stepped in.

Kim closed the door, and still with that heavy silence, headed for the living room. Mitch followed, realizing that her anger was for real and daunting. Other than a few long-ago occasions with his sister, he'd never been around a truly furious woman. His mother had been a lady with a passive nature, sweet and even-tempered. Kim was practically bursting, and he wouldn't have been at all surprised to see steam coming out of her ears.

"Maybe this isn't the best time," he said cautiously. "You're probably tired."

"Yes, I'm tired," Kim retorted sharply, whirling to face him. "I'm tired of pretense and lies. I'm tired of ridiculous denial and an attitude I can't begin to understand. I wish to God I'd never met you, Mitch, and I've walked the floor too many nights and wondered what I ever did that was bad enough to warrant so much punishment."

He felt himself blanch. "That's pretty strong stuff. Do you really mean it?"

"Damned right I mean it!" Kim's eyes were blazing. "I fell so hard for you I couldn't see straight. Lord knew I wasn't thinking straight," she said bitterly. "If there was any way to undo the past month, I'd do it in a heartbeat. I chased you. I forgot every principle I ever lived by and behaved like a sex-starved moron. Never again, Mitch. I'm glad you came by tonight. I'm glad for the chance to—"

He cut in. "To let me have it? Well, just slow down for a minute and let me say something, okay? I'm going to give notice to Armstrong Paving on Monday. Think about that, will you?"

She looked shell-shocked. "You're not serious."

"I'm deadly serious."

Kim turned and walked a harried circle. Her face was screwed up and disapproving when she stopped to look at him again. "You mentioned quitting your job before, and what did I say then? Didn't I let you know how silly I thought that idea was? Do you honestly think I would commend such a foolish solution to a problem that only exists in your own mind?"

But in the back of *her* own mind was a spark of glee. Was he really choosing her over his job? Still, she couldn't and wouldn't let him do it. The problem was his perception of his job, after all, not the job itself.

"I won't be a party to your leaving the company," she added before Mitch could reply. "So if you're thinking that everything would be great between us under those circumstances, think again."

Mitch's eyes narrowed. "Are you saying you wouldn't see me if I quit the company?"

Kim raised her chin for a dramatic announcement. "It's a cowardly way around our problems."

"Cowardly!" The despicable word was a final straw for Mitch. He'd endured her anger without fighting back, thinking that she'd been hurt and deserved to let off a little steam. But calling him cowardly was going too far.

He advanced, slowly, and if his own ears were spurting steam, so be it. "For some reason, you've gotten the wrong impression about me, lady. Anything I've done since we met wasn't because of cowardice. I'm not afraid of Sarge finding out about us, nor am I afraid of anything else you could mention!"

Paling, Kim began backing up. "Uh...you don't have to get so riled," she mumbled. "I didn't say you were cowardly, just your idea."

"It's the same damned thing! Do you grasp the meaning of the word *independence?* Do you see the difference between doing something for yourself and having success handed to you? Can you begin to understand the concept of growing up with very little and working your butt off to better yourself? And on your own, Kim! All by yourself! Without kissing up to the boss or his daughter?"

He was practically in her face. Kim swallowed hard and took a wild stab at bravery. "Don't you dare preach to me. Just who do you think you are?"

"I'll tell you who I am. I'm the guy who can melt your bones with a kiss, lady. I'm the guy you couldn't keep your hands off of the first time we were alone together! Right here under your own roof, if I remember correctly." He snaked out a hand, caught her around the waist and pulled her forward. "Tell me I'm a liar."

"You're a..." The sentence was cut off by a grinding, devouring kiss. Kim's fury hadn't totally dissolved in the face of Mitch's, and it instantly flared at his gall. Sputtering, she pushed against his chest, next pummeling it with her fists.

He held her fast and never broke the kiss. In seconds, she realized that she was neither pushing nor pummeling. Rather, she was breathlessly kissing him back, becoming overheated and excited. Oh, his kisses, she thought weakly.

She could stand toe-to-toe with him and exchange insults all night long, but his kisses destroyed her resistance as though it had never existed.

She felt his hands inside her robe, and they weren't exactly gently. Maybe he was beyond gentleness. Maybe tonight's emotional upheaval had brought him to the point of roughness.

And maybe she liked it. Certainly she was behaving as though she did. While he slid her panties down, she was frantically undoing his belt and fly. Panting and gasping for air, he backed her up to a wall and lifted her. Her legs went around him, willingly, eagerly. His penetration was immediate and took her breath. Clinging to him, kissing his mouth, his chin, his throat, she moaned, "Mitch . . . oh, Mitch."

"Tell me you're through with me," he whispered thickly.

"I can't. I can't." A husky sob escaped. "But don't quit your job . . . please. I won't have that on my conscience."

"I won't do anything you don't want. I promise." His promise was passionate and heartfelt. Right now he would do anything she asked. Right now he loved her more than life itself. Maybe he couldn't say it, but he felt it in every inch of his body, every cell. "Kim . . . sweetheart . . ." The intense pleasure of making love to her, of feeling her special heat and moistness, was making him light-headed. In this they would always connect. In this they were perfect together.

Their urgency grew, their need for completion. "Baby . . . stay with me. I can't hold back."

"I'm with you. Don't stop . . . please don't stop."

Stopping wasn't an option. Speaking normally was out of the question. Their voices were either thin or guttural, barely recognizable imitations of normalcy.

"Kim . . . Kim . . . *Kim!*"

She shuddered and laid her forehead on his shoulder, weakened by the force of her release. Tears seeped from beneath her lashes, emotional tears, tears she couldn't control. Seemingly from a great distance she felt the tremble in Mitch's body. Slowly he let her feet slide to the floor.

They looked at each other. Kim dampened her lips. Mitch's clothes were hanging every which way. Her robe was barely on her body, connected only to her forearms.

And the air was suddenly turbulent with unspoken questions. *Now what? After this, what comes next?*

Ten

An uneasy light shone in Mitch's eyes. He pulled her into his arms with a resigned sigh, cradling her head against his chest. Obviously he couldn't stay away from Kim, whatever problems ensued.

"We'll work it out," he murmured huskily, wondering at the same time just how they would do it. How he would do it. Kim didn't even comprehend his view of their relationship, so how could she offer solutions?

"I've longed to hear you say that," she whispered, lifting her head to see his face. "We can work it out, Mitch, I know we can. It was your unwillingness to try that was destroying me."

His gaze probed hers. "Destroying" might be a little strong, but he knew what she meant. He, too, had been feeling ripped by decisions and circumstances.

She shaped a tremulous smile and brought her hands up to loosen his tie. "You look so handsome in this suit and tie."

He grinned weakly, with some wryness because his suit was wrinkled and his shirttails hanging out. But he said nothing about his own clothing. "I love you in that red dress you wore tonight."

Kim's breath caught. What she would like to hear was *I love* you, *Kim*. Loving her in a left-handed fashion was better than no love, though, and she would settle for what he could give her, when he could give it. With Mitch, she was a shameless, probably foolish woman, and there wasn't one darned thing she could do about it.

But she could love him. Make him happy. Somehow. She shimmied her robe back in place over her shoulders and then snuggled against him, placing her mouth very close to his. That special glint she adored appeared immediately in his eyes, and as she had hoped, he kissed her. It was a kiss of sweetness and profound affection. Indeed, she felt as though her bones were losing rigidity, and the thought made her ecstatically happy.

"It's late and we're both tired," she whispered, hesitating only a moment before adding, "Can you stay?"

Mitch closed his eyes. Was there any longer a point to resistance? Wasn't he putty in Kim's pretty little hands? Apparently he could withdraw a hundred times and he'd still end up right where he was, holding Kim, making love to Kim.

"I can stay," he said, adding with a touch of grimness, "Why not?"

"Yes, why not?" she whispered, wishing immediately that she hadn't responded in that fashion. Neither of them needed another discussion about why they shouldn't be together.

She left him to snap off the living room lamps. "Come," she said softly. He crossed over to her and let her take his hand. Together they walked down the hall to her bedroom.

The bedside lamp was burning and the bed already turned down. Kim helped him off with his jacket, then hung it in her closet. "I'll hang your pants, too. You can put the things from your pockets in that basket on the dresser."

Fishing out his loose change, keys, wallet and handkerchief, he placed them in the basket. Getting out of his pants took only a few seconds, and he silently passed them to Kim. While she matched the leg creases and neatly hung the trousers, he shed his tie, shirt, shoes, socks and underwear.

He climbed into bed and pulled the sheet and summerweight blanket up to his waist. Kim switched off the lamp, let her wrap slide to the floor and crawled in beside him. Their naked bodies melded together, with their arms around each other and their legs tangling.

"This is good," Mitch whispered.

"Very good."

"But I'm suddenly not very tired."

She laughed deep in her throat. "Neither am I."

His right hand began moving under the covers, skimming her waist, the curvature of her hip and thigh, her breasts, where he lingered to caress her nipples, gently, tenderly, touching them as though fascinated by their shape and texture.

Kim's voice dropped to a lower, more intimate level. "Your touch is incredible."

"So is yours." He was referring to the feminine hand invading the most masculine area of his body. His eyes closed with a pleasure that he knew would become demanding if she did that for long. Telling her so never entered his mind, however. He was in heaven, mesmerized by the lady in his arms, who was feathering kisses to his chest. "I love your thighs," he whispered while stroking one from hip to knee.

There was something else he loved, she thought dreamily. Eventually he would admit to loving everything about her, and then she could announce her own feelings. Someday it would happen. Someday everything would be smoothed out and wonderful, and the whole world would know that Mitch Conover and Kim Armstrong were madly in love.

"You have forgotten that idea to quit your job, haven't you?" she murmured.

A slight stiffness entered Mitch's frame. "I'm not sure."

"Mitch..." Kim sat up and peered down at him. Some outside light was filtering through the bedroom curtains, enough to make out his features. "I would never forgive myself if you left the company because of me."

"What do you suggest I do? I'm torn up about sneaking around with you and then trying to look Sarge in the eye. It's got to be one way or the other, Kim. Can't you see that?"

"We could go to Dad together and tell him..."

"No!" Mitch, too, sat up. In the next instant he raked his hair. "Damn, I know he has to be told, but then what will happen? Kim, right now he treats me like he does every other employee. He respects me for my work and that's the end of it. Don't try to convince me that he wouldn't change toward me after finding out about us."

"Change how? In what way? Do you think he would like you less? More? Mitch, I'm leery of using the word, but what are you afraid of?" Kim found his hand and held it, a physical plea for him not to get all macho and bristle because she had again dared to suggest he was afraid of something. "Does the idea of the other men in the company learning about us bother you? Maybe that's it. Maybe it's not Dad at all."

Mitch leaned back against the headboard with a heavy sigh. "It's all of it. I don't want to hear the wisecracks because I'm dating the boss's daughter, and I..."

"You what, Mitch?" she softly urged. "Tell me, please."

"I don't want any favors handed to me on the job because of you."

It finally sunk in. Marveling at her own obtuseness all this time, Kim also leaned against the headboard. "I see." Her thoughts ran wild. Was it possible that Sarge would make things easier for the man she loved? Give him the cushy jobs? Shorten his working hours? Pay him more money? What if she and Mitch got married? Wasn't it only sensible to assume that if her husband was genuinely interested in the company, as Mitch was, Sarge would put him in a position of authority?

Kim's hopes deflated significantly. She couldn't ask her father *not* to promote Mitch, nor would she ever be able to convince Mitch that any promotion he did receive was based entirely on his ability to handle a more difficult job.

"I see it all," she said low and emotionally. "I didn't understand where you were coming from before, but now I do. Very clearly."

Mitch emitted a relieved sigh. "Thank God. Kim, with Morey and Sarge both retiring, there's going to be some drastic reorganization in the company. I think I've got a good chance of moving up. There are three or four other people in the same boat, and the competition is going to be fierce for a while, but I know I stand as good a chance as anyone else."

"I'm sure you do." She thought for a moment. "Mitch, we don't have to tell anyone about us until you're ready. Dad said tonight that his retirement would be announced in the next month or so. You'll know by then exactly where you fit in the new lineup, and . . ."

Mitch broke in. "You'd really do that? You'd keep our relationship private for that long?"

"I'd do almost anything for you, Mitch," she said quietly. And then it came tumbling out, the very words she had vowed to keep buried until Mitch was ready to hear them. "I'm madly, deeply and eternally in love with you. Don't you know that?" There! She'd said it, much sooner than she'd anticipated, and he wasn't leaping out of bed and grabbing his clothes, either. "Say something," she whispered as dread suddenly developed. She had sworn not to push him, and here she was doing it.

"I . . ." He swallowed and licked his lips. Was this really the time? Dare he say it? They weren't only talking about feelings here. Neither had mentioned commitment, but that's what was underlying this conversation.

"Mitch . . . don't leave me hanging like this." Kim gave a feeble, unsteady little laugh.

He took a breath. "I told you I was afraid of nothing, but this scares the hell out of me."

Her heart was pounding hard and fast. "Please don't be scared." She couldn't sit so calmly any longer, and she threw herself across his chest. "Oh, Mitch, say what you feel."

He tried to laugh. Why, he didn't know. She was in his arms. He was holding her, caressing the warm, smooth skin of her back, and the laugh came out as a weak effort. "I never wanted to fall for a princess, Kim."

"It's a pretty word, Mitch, but I'm no princess." She nuzzled her mouth into the undercurve of his jaw. What if he never said it? What if the words forever got stuck in his throat? She knew he loved her, but she needed to hear him say so.

Yet, she also knew something else: Mitch was a private, cautious man, extremely patient when it came to career plans. The time wasn't quite right for him to reveal his personal feelings, and her forcing the issue could turn out bad.

"It's all right," she murmured as another idea formed. The future was lovely to contemplate now. However reticent Mitch was on one crucial subject, he was no longer going to avoid her nor make her feel that she should be avoiding him. They would be seeing each other on a regular basis, and when the shake-up in the company occurred, and Mitch had settled into his new position—he would be one of those moving up, Kim felt certain—then they could go to her parents and tell them everything.

"Mitch..." She stopped. Pinning him down on that point wasn't wise, either, though it had been on the tip of her tongue to do so. "Nothing," she whispered, and added, "Except for this." Wriggling herself around, she straddled his lap. Leaning forward, she pressed her lips to his. "What do you think about this?"

He chuckled softly, enjoyably. "I think you want my body."

Her responsive laugh had a seductive sound. "You're a very bright man." She nipped at his lips with her teeth, until he clasped the back of her head and steadied it for a deep, hungry kiss.

"You're always a surprise," he whispered.

"A good surprise, I hope."

"The best, Kim, the very best." Mitch arranged her hips and legs in a more satisfying position. "Sit down slowly, honey."

The breath whispered out of her as she complied. "Oh, that's good."

"The best, baby, the very best," he growled in her ear.

They slept until nearly noon. Mitch woke up first, realized where he was and turned his head to see Kim. She slept on her side, her back to him. The sheet laid over her, softening the curves of her body. Her long dark hair was tousled and utterly enchanting. *She* was utterly enchanting, an exciting, beautiful woman with a bright mind and a pleasing personality. He was a lucky guy.

Sighing, Mitch lifted his gaze to the ceiling. He was both lucky and unlucky. How had this happened to him? In the past, marriage and having his own family had occasionally crossed his mind, but never could he have imagined himself in this situation. And would it ever change? As long as he and Kim were together, and he stayed with the company, could anything change?

Was he making too much of it? A deep frown furrowed his forehead. Was he being petty and picky and maybe a bit adolescent about his independence? Why was attaining his own success so godawful important? Wouldn't a lot of guys see opportunity in marrying the boss's daughter?

Mitch's mouth tightened. The day he feathered his own nest because of Kim would be a bad day, indeed. His pride would never survive the blow, and a side effect could be the death of the very relationship both he and Kim were trying to protect.

Then, there was the guilt he felt with Sarge. Every time they talked, though their conversations rarely touched on anything but work, he felt like a cheat and a sneak. It was the same with Sara. She had graciously spoken to him last night, complimenting his clothing, chatting about the party and the fine turnout, and every word he'd uttered had felt like deceit. His thoughts would have floored her. *I've been sleeping with your daughter! I think she's in love with me, and I'm more positive by the day that I love her.*

"Damn," Mitch mumbled with abject misery. Falling in love shouldn't make a man miserable. Falling in love should lift a person to the stars. He and Kim should be planning their future, giggling and whispering together. He at least knew that much about serious relationships.

"Mitch?"

He'd been so deeply involved, he hadn't noticed Kim waking up. Turning his head on the pillow, he shaped a smile. "Good morning."

She scooted over to snuggle against him. "Good morning. Have you been awake long?"

His arms went around her. "Just a few minutes." Holding her created a wealth of internal warmth and good feelings. "Did I snore in the night?"

She laughed "If you did, I didn't hear it. Did I?"

He chuckled. "I doubt it."

"You're a kind man." She wriggled closer. "It's nice waking up with you."

"It's nice waking up with you." That much was true. Having Kim in his arms first thing in the morning—regardless that it was really the middle of the day—was the height of pleasure, and he was getting very turned on. The discordant factors of their relationship always felt very far away when he was holding her, he realized.

He was about to kiss her when the phone rang. Kim groaned, but sat up to reach across him. Smiling at him, she said, "Hello," into the phone.

"Hi, honey."

"Mother! I meant to call you this morning. What time is it?" Kim glanced at the clock. "Oh, I didn't know it was so late."

"Are you still in bed? Kim, I'm sorry. It never occurred to me that you might still be sleeping."

"It's all right, Mother. I was awake and just...lying here. Being lazy."

"Did you and Scot talk all night?"

"Half the night, Mother." *The other half... Well, I can't tell you about that. Not yet.* Kim's free hand lifted to caress Mitch's mouth. Tenderly her fingertips played over his lips. He had the most beguiling, sensuous mouth, she thought dreamily while trying to concentrate on her mother's voice.

"We don't have to talk this minute, Kim. Why don't you call me later?"

"Yes... I'll do that. Thanks, Mother." Kim dropped the handset onto the receiver, but she didn't lie down again. Mitch had been nipping at her fingertips, and from the dark, smoldering expression on his face, he was thinking of making love. "I'm going to take a quick shower," she told him. "Don't go away."

His smile connected with her very soul. "Count on it."

Kim bounded from the bed and into the bathroom. Turning on the shower so the spray would warm up, she brushed her teeth and then found a new toothbrush for Mitch to use, which she laid, still in its packaging, next to the sink.

Then she entered the shower and closed the glass door behind her.

Mitch waited until he was sure Kim was in the shower, then walked in calling, "Want some company?"

Kim giggled. "I'd love some company."

Mitch spotted the new toothbrush. "Give me a minute." Quickly he brushed his teeth. He opened the shower door. "Hey, looks wet in there." It also looked inviting. Kim's hair was slicked back, and water was running down her luscious body.

He stepped in with a suggestive waggle of his eyebrows. "I'll wash yours if you wash mine."

"Mine's already washed," she quipped with a deliberately leering glance that swept down his chest and belly. "But I'd love to wash yours."

Their fun in the shower delighted Kim. When Mitch wasn't worrying himself to death, he was a real sweetheart.

Her love for him just kept expanding, she thought happily while they dried each other with big towels.

"Breakfast or...?" She let the implication dangle.

He pulled her damp body against his. "What do you think?"

Breakfast took place an hour and a half later.

That day and evening were the most pleasant and pleasurable in Kim's memory. They cooked, ate, took a long walk, laughed over the silliest things, ate again and made love. Mitch said he'd better be on his way around nine that night. They were going to maintain their separate residences, and Mitch had to be up very early on workday mornings. Kim's schedule wasn't quite so regimented, but she, too, took Mondays seriously.

They stood in her foyer to say good-night. "The day was wonderful," she murmured with stars in her eyes. "Come here after work tomorrow, for dinner."

Mitch pulled her forward for a kiss, which he administered with a touching tenderness. "I have a class tomorrow night, Kim."

"Oh. Sorry. I'd forgotten. How late will you be?"

"The class is over at nine-thirty. I'd like to stop by, but I really should go home then."

How disappointing. But his routines were as important to him as hers were to her. "Yes, of course. Do you have any evenings free during the week?"

"Wednesdays."

She bravely smiled. "On Wednesday I'll prepare a feast." Her left eyebrow arched. "I expect you'll be hungry by Wednesday."

"Ravenous," he whispered huskily, and they both knew the topic under discussion wasn't food. He hugged her, tightly, almost roughly. Someday, he suspected, they wouldn't be saying goodbye on Sunday night, nor reining in their emotions for three days of abstinence. If ever there were two people who needed to be together on a permanent basis, it was him and Kim. Obviously she didn't want him to leave, and the ache in his gut because he had to was reminder enough of his own preference on the matter.

Her arms were around his waist, her breasts pressing into his chest. She was wearing a skirt and, he already knew, no panties. They had made love twice last night and twice since waking up at noon, and holding her for what had started as a simple good-night kiss was arousing him again.

"Damn, you're something," he whispered.

"So you've said before," she whispered back, knowing precisely to what he was referring. "Wanna know a secret, handsome? There have been times—not many, but a few— when I've wondered if I weren't a little cold where men are concerned."

"You, cold?" he scoffed. "Baby, if you were any hotter, I wouldn't have the strength to walk to my truck."

She chuckled into his shirt. "Is walking what interests you right now?"

"I think you know what interests me right now." His hands slid down her back to her hips, where he began bunching up her skirt. Her sexually charged sigh when he found bare skin darted through him like a shot of adrenaline. "Kim..." Seeking her lips, he bestowed a passionate, suddenly needful kiss, thrusting his tongue into her mouth.

She writhed and rubbed against him. "Oh, Mitch, you turn my knees to mush." Her hands unlocked behind him to glide to his belt buckle and zipper.

"Just a second," he growled, and bent slightly to scoop her off the floor and into his arms. "Let's do this right."

She laughed, throatily, happily, during the short trip to her bedroom.

Mitch left at ten-fifteen. Then, and only then, did she remember her promise to call her mother. Was it too late? Frowning, Kim sat at the living room phone and dialed her parents' number.

Sara answered. "Hello?"

"Mother, if you and Dad are in bed, I can call in the morning."

"We're in bed, Kim, but we've been watching television. I'm glad you called. Is everything all right?"

"Everything's fine. I didn't call earlier because I got tied up." *Tied up in Mitch's arms.* Kim bit her lip. She hated keeping important facts from her parents, and nothing else in her adult life had ever been so important. She especially wanted to share her happiness with her mother. She and Sara had always been very close, and in all honesty, there had never before been an occasion when she couldn't tell her mother every tiny detail of her daily existence.

"With a client?" Sara asked.

"Um...yes, with a client." An out-and-out lie. Kim's discomfort magnified. "How's Dad? The party went well, I thought. What does he think?"

"I'll let him tell you." Kim could hear the phone being passed and her mother's voice. "Kim wants to know what you thought of the party."

Sarge came on the line. "Hi, baby."

"Hi, Dad. What I was really wondering about was your retirement announcement. Are you serious about retiring?"

Sarge chuckled. "I'd better be. Your mother wants to do some traveling, and if I'm not free soon, she's apt to go off without me."

Sara's voice reached Kim's ears. "Sarge, that's not true. Stop planting disruptive seeds in our daughter's mind."

"I'm not worried," Kim assured her father. "Not about you two."

"You shouldn't be," Sarge told her. "Your mother and I will be together till death do us part."

It was exactly the way she felt about Mitch, Kim thought, visualizing herself and Mitch watching television in bed together thirty years from now, and maybe talking on the phone to one of their children. She sighed.

"Anyway," Sarge elaborated, "I am serious about retirement, Kim. Next year at this time, your mother and I'll probably be on the other side of the globe. Think you can handle that okay, honey?"

"Of course I can handle it. Don't give it a thought. Uh, Dad, when do you think you'll be making your announcement?"

"In a few weeks. I've got to get things lined up with the company, Kim. Morey's retirement gave me a start, no two ways about it. I've leaned on Morey for a long time, and now someone's not only going to have to take his place, I've got to choose the right person to fill my shoes."

"No one can fill your shoes, Dad."

"That's nice to hear, honey, but it's highly unrealistic. No one's indispensable."

Kim laughed lightly. "You come close."

After ten minutes of the usual family chitchat, Kim said good-night and hung up. She sat in the silence of her condo and mulled things over. Her promise to Mitch to keep their relationship private until after Sarge's retirement was already pinching. She could make things so easy for the man she loved and hoped to marry. Sarge would be surprised to learn of their involvement, but how could she doubt her father's cooperation and possibly even his eagerness to help?

But a promise was a promise, and not only that, going behind Mitch's back was not the way to begin a lifelong commitment. As much as she wanted to confide in her parents, she would keep silent and let Mitch handle his career.

Oddly, Mitch, too, was on the phone with family. The telephone had been ringing when he walked into his apartment, and he'd grabbed it, thinking it was Kim.

But it was Blair, his sister in Montana. "Mitch, you devil! I've been calling all day. Are you all right?"

"I'm fine. Are you all right?"

"Never better. I've been trying to get hold of you to give you some great news. Mitch, I'm pregnant."

"Blair, that's fantastic!"

"Yes, it is. Mitch, I'm so happy. Ace is wonderful, the best husband in the world. I love living on his ranch—our ranch, he keeps reminding me—and now we're going to have a baby."

"I'm glad, Blair. Incidentally, I met someone important, too." Mitch winced. He hadn't intended mentioning Kim to anyone, yet, certainly not to his sister who would try to pry every minuscule detail out of him.

"You did? Tell me about her! Is she pretty? Intelligent? Oh, I know she is. When can I meet her? Can she come home with you next month? Oh, bring her, Mitch, please."

Next month? His vacation! He'd forgotten all about his vacation! It was less than a month away, more like three weeks, and with what was going on in the company at the present, not the most auspicious time to be taking two weeks off.

"We'll see," he said vaguely, wondering in the back of his mind if he shouldn't rearrange his vacation schedule. "Tell me about the ranch, Toad." Toad was his pet name for Blair. As a girl she had screeched at him whenever he used it, but she seemed to like it now.

The ploy worked. Blair launched into a recitation of the ranch's many good qualities. They hung up twenty minutes later, with Blair insisting one more time that he bring his girlfriend along on his vacation.

Exhausted then, Mitch crawled into bed. Rubbing his tired eyes he mentally put a period to the weekend. Tomorrow was Monday. He would see Kim on Wednesday. The other evenings would be taken up with classes.

And he couldn't begin to imagine what would take place during the week's working hours. No, all he could do about those hours was hope that Sarge Armstrong wouldn't overlook Mitch Conover when he began handing out promotions.

Then . . . after that . . . once the reorganization had occurred and the dust had settled . . . he and Kim . . .

Mitch's thoughts faded into the obscurity of a deep and mindless sleep.

Eleven

After two weeks Kim was a bundle of nerves. When was her father going to announce his retirement? When was Mitch going to learn who had been promoted in the company, and who hadn't?

She called her mother regularly, hoping to hear a hint of company gossip, discreetly asking questions and getting nowhere as Sara apparently knew no more about what was happening than she did.

Mitch, too, was on edge. They spent Wednesday evenings together, and the weekends, and each of them was trying hard to appear normal and without strain, though it was obvious neither was succeeding very well.

On edge or not, being together was exciting. As promised, Kim had a wonderful meal prepared that first Wednesday. They kissed and hugged when Mitch arrived, then sat down at the table and attempted to conceal their anticipation of the evening ahead.

"So," Kim said with studied nonchalance. "How's the job going?"

Mitch knew she wasn't referring to his current paving project. "There's nothing new, Kim. No one in the lower ranks knows anything."

They fell into a brooding silence until Mitch complimented the food. "Great chicken, Kim."

"Thank you." It was an absentminded response. Kim really wanted to shout, *What's taking so damned long?* But it was her own father who was "taking so damned long," and she could hardly suggest—especially to Mitch—that Sarge Armstrong was dragging his heels. After all, hadn't the mere idea of his retirement taken her and everyone else by surprise? Maybe he'd changed his mind and just hadn't let her know. Maybe nothing was going to happen within Armstrong Paving's lineup. Maybe she was waiting and worrying and slowly going crazy for no reason at all!

She held her tongue on that perturbing notion all evening on Wednesday, managed the same silence throughout the weekend, succeeded—just barely—in staying quiet about it the following Wednesday and tried very hard to do so during the second weekend.

But the tension she was enduring came through in bed on Saturday night. "What's wrong?" Mitch questioned afterward, while leaning on an elbow to look down into her face. "Are you all right?"

Kim slowly inhaled. "What I am is slightly bonkers," she finally confessed. "Aren't you?" She searched his eyes for the truth.

"It's not easy," Mitch admitted, lying back to stare at the ceiling.

"Mitch...what if nothing happens?" There was an uncertain quaver in her voice. He didn't answer. "Have you thought of that possibility?"

"I believe something will happen."

His stubbornness made Kim sigh. "Fine, but don't you think we should consider the alternative? I have no solid reason to suspect anything other than what Dad said, but what if he changes his mind about retirement and then decides that the company's present personnel can do just fine without Morey? Maybe there aren't going to be any promotions."

"Kim..."

He'd said her name with a discouraged helplessness, alarming Kim. Planting doubts wasn't her intention.

But what was?

Kim frowned. Always, eternally, she kept wanting Mitch to be different than he was. On only one subject, of course. Other than his determined goal of autonomous success, Mitch was perfect. His refusal to discuss alternatives was a jarring note, but no one ever changed another person's innate traits and attitudes by harping on them. Turning into a nag was the worst thing she could do, and, sad to say, that was where she was heading.

"I'm sorry, Mitch," she whispered, emotionally shaken by the frustration of waiting for an event that was beyond her control. Actually, she could do quite a lot to make things easier for everyone concerned—for Mitch, in particular— and staying out of it was really at the heart of her frustration. But interference was a risk she wasn't quite brave enough to take.

"Maybe we'll hear something next week," she added, speaking hopefully. In the meantime, they had tonight and tomorrow together. She had arranged her appointments and commitments so the weekend would be completely free. Julie Hildebrand's white bedroom suite was coming along nicely, as were Kim's other projects. Omitting weekend appointments from her calendar overloaded her evenings during the week, but with Mitch so involved in his classes, it was best that she plan her time to coincide with his schedule.

It was also time she hired that assistant she'd been considering for so long. Fourteen-hour days and hectic weekends no longer held any appeal. When Mitch had free time, she wanted to be available, and he had told her last Sunday that his current classes would be completed in another week.

"Kim..."

"Yes?" The bedside lamp was on. They only made love in the dark now if they happened to awaken in the night. Looking at his profile warmed Kim's soul and flooded her system with love.

"I changed my vacation from August to October," he said.

Kim raised up to an elbow. "Isn't your sister expecting you in August?"

"She was, yes. I called her and explained." Mitch's gaze dropped from the ceiling to Kim's face. "I can't be gone for two weeks right now."

"No, I suppose you can't." He hadn't asked her to go with him for those two weeks, even though she had suggested it herself—only in fun, of course—the first time he'd come to her condo. The painful truth was that Mitch hadn't committed himself as totally to her as she had to him. Sarge's retirement was an enormous mark in the progress of their relationship, more like a pushing off point for Mitch.

Or, at least, that was how she prayed he viewed it. Pondering, uneasily, the many unknowns still lurking within their affiliation, Kim lay back.

"What are you thinking?" Mitch asked, speaking softly.

"About us. About how much I love you." He'd never said it, not once, and she would gladly give up her business to hear him say it right now. *Kim, I love you, too.*

Kim's mood was clear to Mitch, but the timing wasn't right and the words simply would not come out of his mouth. Next week, maybe. Or the week after. What did he have to offer her right now? Admitting love would just naturally lead to a marriage proposal. That was how he thought, how he believed. Falling in love with a woman of Kim's caliber led to marriage.

And what if her speculation is right and nothing happens in the company? What if three months from now you're still a project supervisor? Will you ask her to marry you then?

Mitch's mouth went dry, his heart beating like a tom-tom. That was the sixty-four-dollar question, and it made him sweat every time it blasted his mind.

They laid there, each mired in disturbing thoughts. The future was vague, obscure, joyful to contemplate one minute, painful the next.

He couldn't do this to Kim any longer, Mitch thought unhappily. He was in her bed at every opportunity, and that wasn't going to change whatever happened in the company. He at least owed her his honesty.

"I... love you, too," he said, albeit in a soft voice.

Kim's eyes got as big as saucers. Had she heard him right? "Pardon?"

"I said, I love you, too." His voice was a little stronger.

"You didn't want to say it."

"No, I didn't."

"Then why did you?"

Startled because she sounded more angry than anything else, he reared up and peered down at her. "Am I missing something here? Are you mad at me?"

Tears began seeping from the corners of her eyes. "Oh, Mitch, it's all so hopeless." Why was she crying now? Hadn't she, not more than two minutes ago, been willing to trade her successful business for those words? He'd said it. He had actually come right out and told her he loved her. What more did she want?

"I'm sorry," she whispered tearily. "I wanted to hear your feelings so badly, and now I'm ruining everything."

"You're ruining nothing. Try to be patient, Kim." Leaning over her, Mitch began caressing her face, her cheek, the curve of her throat. "I'm glad I said it. I love you, and I should have told you weeks ago."

"Oh, Mitch, I love you...so very, very much." Her voice was a tear-clogged croak, rusty sounding, cracking with emotion. She tried to smile. "It hurts, doesn't it?"

He nodded. "Yeah, it hurts. Now I should be asking you to marry me, and I can't. Not yet."

"But you're thinking about it."

"I'm thinking about it, yes." Mitch bent his head to kiss her lips. The contact sent shock waves through his system, and he settled his mouth on hers in a more satisfying position. Her lips were moist and yielding. Her arms went up around his neck, and the kiss lasted until they were both breathless and needing more than kisses.

She urged him into the cradle of her thighs. "Make love to me with love on your mind," she whispered. "Right now we're the only two people on the planet. Do you feel it?"

"I feel it." He slid into her heat. "You will always be the only woman in the world for me, Kim. Believe it."

"I do... Oh, I do."

"Hey, Conover!"

Mitch looked over to the voice and saw a young man in a suit. He recognized Jim Sutton picking his way through men, equipment and materials, coming toward him. Mitch's eyes narrowed. Sutton worked in the office, in personnel, and his appearance at a job site could mean just about anything.

Picking up a rag from an open toolbox, Mitch wiped his hands. Sutton arrived. "I have a message for you."

Mitch tossed the rag. "What is it?"

"Sarge wants you to join him for lunch, at twelve-thirty."

"Today?" He was dirty. His clothes were dirty. And it was nearly twelve, not enough time to drive home for a shower and a change.

"Yes, today. He said to come as you are. You'll be eating in Sarge's office."

"Oh, that's different. All right, thanks. I'll be there."

Sutton looked around. "Looks like this job is almost finished."

Mitch nodded. "Another day should do it." They were paving a modest parking lot, a small job. A large project was coming up, however, thirty miles of interstate in northern California. Mitch would be away from Seattle for weeks, which he wasn't looking forward to. His classes were coming to an end, but he hated being away from Kim for that long.

Still, that was the paving business. A contractor moved men, equipment and material to the job site, which could take him clear across the country for extended periods of time, months, in some cases. As long as he remained a project supervisor, Mitch knew there would be separations for him and Kim to deal with.

After Jim Sutton left, Mitch went to a nearby gas station and washed up in its rest room. It was the best he could do in the few minutes he had, and it was accomplished with a knot of anxiety in his gut. This could be it, the moment he'd been waiting for. If there was no promotion in his immediate future, he'd be leaving Sarge's office in a real quandary, as breaking off with Kim was no longer an option.

He drove to company headquarters, parked his truck and ambled into the building as though he did it every day. The receptionist greeted him, a woman he didn't know.

"May I help you?"

"I'm Mitch Conover. Sarge sent for me."

"Oh, yes. I have it written down right here. You're to go directly to Mr. Armstrong's office. Do you know where it is?"

"Yes, thanks."

Sarge's office was on the second floor. Mitch's tension magnified during the short elevator ride. Obviously Sarge had something to say to him, but what?

He rapped on the door and heard, "Come in." Sarge got up from his desk and came forward with his hand outstretched. "Mitch, good of you to come." They shook hands. "Sit down. Lunch will be here shortly."

They sat down, Sarge on one side of the desk, Mitch on the other. Sarge smiled. "You're probably wondering why I called you in."

Mitch nodded. "Business, I expect."

"Business, yes, but not a new project." He chuckled. "Well, I guess it is a new project, but not at all what you're used to. Before I get to that, let me ask you something, Mitch. How do you feel about the company?"

"Any company is only as good as the man who runs it, Sarge. You've made Armstrong Paving a good place to work. I like my job, and I have a lot of respect for you and for the company in general.''

"And you plan to stay with us for a long time?"

"Forever, if you'll have me."

"That's what I thought."

Sarge was still smiling, Mitch noted. His own pulse was beating rapidly, anxiously. Sarge was going to impart some important news, and a portion of it was going to touch on him.

"Well . . . my retirement is a certainty, Mitch. I plan to be out of this office by the end of the year." Sarge got up and walked around the desk to sit on a corner of it. "Mitch, I've studied every man in the company with a fine-tooth comb. I've looked at small things, like absenteeism, to major data, such as how they get along with the other employees, and personality traits, and ambition and determination."

Not knowing where this was going, Mitch merely nodded. Sarge continued. "There are other factors, of course, which I won't go into right now, but it was a weeding out process. I wanted someone already in the company, I'm sure you can understand, someone with both feet on the ground, someone trainable."

"Trainable?" Where *was* this going? Was Sarge talking about him?

"I wanted someone young, Mitch, someone who didn't hesitate to give up his evenings to further himself. This company means a great deal to me. Someday my daughter will inherit it, and I want there to be something left for her to inherit. You know my daughter, don't you?"

Mitch wanted to sink through the floor. "Uh . . . yes."

Sarge's smile got a yard wide. "You're it, Mitch, if you want the job. You're the man to occupy this office."

It didn't immediately register, and when it did, Mitch felt the blood drain from his head. "Me?"

"Yes, you."

"Why?" Even if he sounded ungrateful, Mitch couldn't stifle the question. Why him? There were others who'd been with the company much longer, men and women who'd already spent years in administration. This didn't make sense.

"Because you're like me, Mitch. Out of all my employees, you're the one who reminds me of myself at your age. I did everything I could to get somewhere, and I remember those days very well. I've had my eye on you for a long time, and even without my retirement, you would have been brought into administration."

"But your job, Sarge. My God, what do I know about running the company?"

"Very little right now, I expect." Sarge chuckled. "By the time I leave, you'll know my routines inside and out. Believe me, I don't run this place by myself. We have great people in sales and in every other department, and you'll rely on them, as I do. Incidentally, you'll be very well paid."

Mitch cleared his throat. "I don't know what to say."

"Say you'll take it," Sarge boomed jovially.

"I...I'll take it. Of course I'll take it. I never expected..."

Two hours later, Mitch walked out of the building in a daze. He would start in the morning, coming here instead of to his present project. Sarge would train him himself, show him the ropes, was the way Sarge had put it. He'd slapped Mitch on the back and shaken his hand again at the door. Mitch had thanked him, profusely.

Now, heading home—Sarge had told him to go home for the rest of the day—Mitch rehashed every small detail of the last several hours. This was incredible, so much more than he'd dared hope for. Had he honestly ever hoped to sit in Sarge Armstrong's chair? No, his imagination had never taken him that far.

Kim. He had to tell Kim. Mitch took note of where he was and made a right turn to alter his course. Just last Sunday afternoon she had brought him to her studio. He'd sensed her pride in the place and in her own accomplishments, which she was very entitled to feel. Kim was like Sarge, ambitious, intelligent and successful.

Mitch smiled. Sarge's opinion that he was like him was a compliment of the highest order. He would do his utmost to live up to that opinion. Sarge would never have cause to be disappointed in Mitch Conover.

But still... it seemed more like a dream than reality. He was the new head of Armstrong Paving! Mitch's gusto erupted, and he laughed and slapped the steering wheel. This would knock Kim's shoes off! And his sister's.

Reaching the building in which Kim's studio took up a corner, Mitch parked the truck and got out whistling. The whistle died when he saw the sign on the studio door: Closed. Disappointed, he returned to his truck.

Only he didn't immediately drive away and head for Kim's condo. The meeting with Sarge kept running through his mind. *You're it, Mitch, if you want the job. You know my daughter, don't you? I want someone already in the company. You remind me of myself at your age. You know my daughter. My daughter... my daughter...*

A scene suddenly appeared behind Mitch's eyes. Kim and Sarge together, talking. *Dad, I've been meaning to tell you something for weeks now. Mitch Conover and I are in love. We'd like to be married, but Mitch is concerned about his job. Could you possibly move him up so that he stops worrying? He's had this silly idea about getting involved with the boss's daughter, and he must never know I talked to you like this. But can you do something, Dad?*

And Sarge saying, *Honey, for you, anything. I'll advance him so far, there'll never be another reason for him to worry about his future.*

No! Kim wouldn't do that. She'd volunteered to keep their relationship private. She wouldn't... she wouldn't...

But neither was she happy—nor patient—because things had been moving so slowly. And God knew she'd been worrying about what they would do if Mitch wasn't promoted.

Shaken, Mitch started the truck. His stomach was churning sickishly. Why else would Sarge elevate a man from so far down in the ranks? Skipping a few steps in the advance-

ment game would have been a lot more understandable.
Being handed the top job in the company, Sarge's own position, was ludicrous, preposterous. Things like this didn't
happen to ordinary people, and there was only one fact in
his whole damned existence that made him at all extraordi-
nary: Kim!

Mitch drove with his mind split between the road and the
anger building in his system. His conclusion was only sensible. Kim had spilled the beans, whether deliberately or
unintentionally, and Sarge, being a doting father, had reacted exactly as Mitch had feared. He hadn't earned his
promotion at all—how in hell could he have?—and he
wasn't going to accept it. He'd tell Sarge face-to-face,
probably in the morning, but he'd tell Kim face-to-face today.

Her car wasn't parked within her condo compound, and
grim-faced, stony-eyed, Mitch made the decision to wait
right there for Kim to get home, however long it took.

It had been a hectic day. Kim had kept appointments with
three new clients, interviewed two women for the assistant's job, spent over an hour at her desk ordering materials for several projects and delivered a carton of recently
finished throw pillows—white satin and silk—to Julie Hildebrand.

Mrs. Hildebrand gushed every time she saw Kim. "It's
turning into the most gorgeous bedroom suite I've ever seen.
I've recommended you to a dozen of my friends, Kim."

Kim always thanked Mrs. Hildebrand. Word-of-mouth
was really the best advertising she could have, and a truly
satisfied customer never failed to bring in additional business.

But "additional business" wasn't uppermost in Kim's
mind these days. An assistant would ease the burden, of
course, and so far she had interviewed five people for the
job. One of them, a young man, stood out. His name was
Michael Branson. And though she had stressed the part-time

status of the position and the modest salary, Michael had remained enthusiastic.

Everything else going on was superfluous, Kim thought again with a heavy sigh. Today was Wednesday, which meant she would see Mitch this evening, but she wanted to see him every single day, every morning, every night. She wanted to be with him all the time, to eat her meals with him, to talk with him, share quiet moments with him, to have him within reach all night, every night.

She wanted to be married to him, to be Mrs. Mitch Conover. God, would it really happen someday? Was she too impatient? Too anxious? Why did she constantly feel that something was going to snatch Mitch away? Some awful incident that she couldn't possibly foresee and prevent?

After stopping at a supermarket for groceries, Kim drove home. Mitch's pickup parked near her condo surprised her.

But it also pleased her. He must have gotten off work early today and come right over.

She got out with a smile and a cheerful yell. "Hi! Come and help me haul in the grub I bought."

Mitch was already climbing out. He walked over to her, and when she turned up her face for a kiss, he bypassed her mouth and cooly brushed her cheek with his lips.

"Hey, that's no way to greet the woman you love," Kim teased.

Turning away, Mitch reached for the grocery sacks in her back seat.

Kim frowned. "Are you in a bad mood, or something?"

"We'll talk inside."

The chill in his voice was frightening. "Mitch . . . what's wrong?"

Picking up three sacks, he walked away. Scrambling for the last remaining sack, Kim hurriedly closed the car door and raced after him. She quickly unlocked the condo door and went in, with Mitch on her heels. They carried the food to the kitchen. "Just set those sacks on the table," she mumbled while doing the same with the one she'd carried in, as well as her purse.

"Now…" She turned to face him. "What's wrong?" Her heart nearly stopped at the icy expression in Mitch's blue eyes.

He took a belligerent stance, his feet apart, his hands on his hips. "Sarge called me into his office today. For lunch and a chat."

"He did?" Excitement suddenly welled in Kim. "Did he … oh, Mitch, did he give you a promotion? Is his retirement official?"

"Yes to both questions."

"And?" She could hardly contain herself, but then Mitch's coldness sank in again. "Wait." Her voice had become thready and terribly shaky. "Something's very wrong. You're not happy with whatever Dad said to you. What was it?"

"I think you already know."

Kim blinked. "How would I know? I talked to Mother yesterday, but she didn't tell me anything."

"When did you last talk to your dad?"

"I don't know. Two or three mights ago, I guess." She remembered. "On Monday night. Why? Mitch, you certainly don't think he told me his plans and I kept them from you, do you?"

"What I think you did was tell him about us."

Her mouth dropped open. "I didn't!"

"Then why in hell did he give me his job?" Mitch snarled.

His anger was intimidating, but what he'd just announced nearly floored her. "He gave you *his* job? You mean, he promoted you to head of the company?"

Her innocence rubbed Mitch wrong. The more he thought about it, the more convinced he was of her deceit. Sarge hadn't handed him the most responsible job in the company for no reason. The highest-paid position Armstrong Paving had to offer, the most respected? No way.

"You're lying, Kim."

The air whooshed out of her. "Don't do this, Mitch. I'm *not* lying. I never said a word to either Mother or Dad. Ask them, if you don't believe me."

"Oh, I will, make no mistake."

Her own anger was flaring. "Do it now! Call them right now!"

"Not on the phone. I want to do this face-to-face!"

"Do what?"

Mitch's face was dark with fury. "What the hell do you think? I told you a hundred times I wouldn't take favors because of you. Did you think I wouldn't figure it out? Did Sarge? You might think I'm stupid, Kim, but I'm not."

"The hell you're not!" she shrieked. "I had nothing to do with that promotion, but go ahead and ruin everything, if that's what you're so bent on doing! Quit your job! Go to Dad and tell him what you think, and he'll probably can your butt even if you don't quit! It's what you deserve, you . . . you jerk!"

Kim collapsed then, leaning against the refrigerator to sob out her misery. The very best had happened and Mitch wouldn't accept it. She was weary of the game, tired of secrecy, tired of everything. "Just get the hell out of here," she choked out. "You have no more faith in me than you'd have in a total stranger. I'm through, Mitch."

He hadn't expected this, but then what had he expected? Had he thought Kim would wilt and confess what she'd done? She wasn't the wilting kind of woman. Besides, he'd known it was over before she'd said it. No relationship could withstand this sort of pressure.

"So long, babe," he said with heavy sarcasm, which was out of character for him; but it was either sarcasm or tears at this awful moment.

Her teary eyes shot him a murderous look and she turned her back.

Mitch hesitated. Walking out now would guarantee the demise of their relationship, the end of their love, the finish line. "Damn," he muttered under his breath. Was this what he wanted?

It wasn't, but how could be back off now?

Squaring his shoulders, he made a swift and determined exit.

Twelve

Mitch stewed all night, but he couldn't believe he'd earned that promotion, no matter how passionately he wished it were true. One small hope sprouted sometime between midnight and dawn: maybe Sarge had learned of him and Kim's involvement from another source. Maybe Kim hadn't said anything about it, and maybe he'd dealt her an unfair blow.

He almost called her, at one, at two, at four. Was she rolling and tossing, too? Was she as miserable as he was? He thought of her in bed, naked, soft, warm, and broke out in a sweat. If he didn't get this mess straightened out, he would never hold her again. But was it possible to make everyone happy? He couldn't take Sarge's job, and Kim would probably never forgive him for that, even if everything else settled down.

He was up at daybreak, and showered, shaved and dressed by six. At six-thirty he left for the drive across town to the Armstrong building, and at seven he pulled into the parking lot. Only a handful of vehicles were occupying spaces.

The building was open. A few people were at their desks. Mitch said hello and took the elevator to the second floor. Sarge was in his office. He looked up from his desk with a pleased smile. "I knew you'd be an early bird, Mitch. Come on in. We can get started immediately. Right now I'm—"

"Wait, Sarge. There's something that needs discussion before we go any further."

Sarge sat back, looking comfortably at ease. "Let it out, Mitch. Always feel free to talk to me about anything. There's coffee over there on that table, if you want some."

"No, thanks."

"Sit down, Mitch. Whatever it is, you don't have to stand there looking like a man awaiting his own execution."

It was a joke, Mitch realized. But he didn't feel like laughing. This was no laughing matter, not for him and not for Kim.

Still, he relaxed enough to sit down. "It's about Kim."

Sarge became very still, though he leaned forward a little. "What about Kim?"

"Actually, it's about Kim and me."

"Go on."

Was he surprised? It was hard to tell with Sarge, Mitch realized. Sarge Armstrong was nobody's fool, and if he didn't want to give away his thoughts, no one would see them in his eyes or on his face.

"I'm sure she told you," Mitch said quietly. Smoothly, he hoped.

"Told me what, Mitch?"

"You have to know, Sarge. Why else would you have kicked me so far upstairs?"

Sarge slowly sat back in his chair. "So that's it." His eyes had narrowed some and his steady, unblinking gaze rested solidly on Mitch's face. "You've been second-guessing my decision, and the only reason you can find for your advancement is your relationship with my daughter. Tell me about that, Mitch. What sort of relationship do you have with Kim?"

"Sarge . . . you had to know."

Sarge's eyes suddenly blazed. "Like hell I did! Fill me in, Mitch. And don't leave out the part about my own daughter keeping me in the dark."

Mitch felt himself go pale. "If you really didn't know, why did I get the best job in the company?"

"Because you deserved it!" Sarge roared. "I wanted young blood and ambition in this office! Do you know what every other unmarried man in the company does with his evenings? I'll tell you what they do. They hang out in bars, they drink, they chase women! Don't get me wrong. I enjoy a good drink as well as any man, and I've never been accused of disliking women. But no one—no one, Mitch— on my payroll gives two hoots about furthering his education, except you."

"You gave me your job because of a few classes?"

"I gave you my job because you have the guts and intelligence to want something better!" Sarge drew a breath. "This thing with Kim makes a difference, though. Why didn't she tell her mother and me about the two of you?"

Mitch dampened his dry lips. "I . . . asked her not to."

"Why?" The word was snapped out and stingingly sharp.

Mitch felt sick to his stomach. "I . . . didn't want any favoritism."

"And you thought I would favor you above the other men because you were courting Kim? You damned fool."

That is exactly what I am, Mitch thought, a damned fool.

"Clarify a point for me, Conover. You were courting Kim with something honorable in mind, weren't you?"

"Uh . . . yes. Yes, of course," he stammered.

"Have you asked her to marry you?"

"Uh . . . no."

"And you call that honorable?" Disgustedly, Sarge picked up a pen and, after a second, threw it down again. "Well . . . this is a fine kettle of fish. Tell you what, Mitch. You go home and think about our little conversation. If you absolutely cannot accept your own value to me and to this company, I suggest you hit the road. Is that clear enough?"

"Yes, sir." Mitch stumbled to his feet. Never in his life had he made a more horrifying mistake. He had misjudged both Kim and Sarge. Worse than that, he'd misjudged himself. He'd earned that terrific promotion by being himself, a man with ambition and the tenacity to do something about it, a man who wasn't afraid of hard work nor objected to biding his time for opportunity.

And then, in the wink of an eye, he'd destroyed all he'd gained, his relationship with Kim, his good job, Sarge's faith in him, *Kim's* faith in him.

His lips felt too numb to speak, and his words tumbled over each other. "Do you object to my seeing Kim after this?"

"Kim's a grown woman," Sarge growled. "She'll see who she wants, when she wants." He cocked an eyebrow. "Are you asking for my approval?"

"I am."

"That's a new one. Do young men ask for a father's approval these days?" Sarge's face hardened again. "Did you ask for my approval before? How long have you and Kim been seeing each other?"

"Since we met at your house the night you had me over for dinner."

"That long?" Sarge sighed. "I wish Kim had told me." He hit Mitch with a harsh look. "I wish you had told me."

Mitch nervously shifted his weight. "I should have. I'm sorry."

"Yeah, right. Go on, get the hell out of here. I've got work to do."

Mitch started for the door. But he stopped halfway and turned. "Sarge, do I still have a job?"

Sarge stared a hole in him. "Come back tomorrow, Mitch. Let's let it simmer for a day and talk again in the morning."

Feeling lower than a snake's belly, Mitch exited Sarge's office and stumbled to the elevator. How could he have been such an idiot? Kim had fallen in love with him. He'd fallen for her, hard, and almost from their first meeting. Then Sarge, completely in the dark, had handed him the most exciting opportunity of his life, and he'd thanked him by throwing it back in his face. He'd botched everything.

A glance at his watch was surprising. It was still early, barely seven-thirty. So much had happened, and it seemed more like hours than minutes since he'd walked into Sarge's office.

Kim would still be at home. He had to see her, had to apologize, explain, beg for forgiveness. God, if she wouldn't listen, what would he do?

Tearing off his tie and suit coat, he jumped into his truck and then drove through the morning rush-hour traffic, muttering curses. People drove like fools to get to work, and did it again at night to get home. He was no better. No bigger fool had ever lived. If Sarge didn't want him now, he couldn't blame the man, but the prospect of starting over with another company made him feel nauseous. It was all so unnecessary, and maybe that's what Kim had been trying to tell him all along.

He got out at her condo and walked to her door on leaden feet. The doorbell echoed from within, and he waited anxiously for the door to open.

Instead, Kim's voice came through. "I don't want to see you, Mitch."

"Kim...please. Just for a minute."

The doorbell had awakened Kim. Her eyes felt swollen from crying half the night, and the other half had passed in a restless, fitful semiconsciousness. "Go away!"

"I'm not going away!" Mitch pounded on the door with his fist. "You've got to see me!"

"I don't have to do any such thing! You said your piece last night, and I don't want to hear any more of it!"

"Kim, I just saw Sarge. Please...I was so wrong. Please let me come in."

So much shouting was bound to alert the neighbors. Besides, despite her bravado last night, Mitch talking to her father was troubling. What had he told Sarge about them? Would her parents be hurt because she'd been so secretive?

Kim yanked open the door. "Go and sit in the living room while I wash my face."

Mitch watched her stalking off, her robe billowing out behind her. She was ticked and he didn't blame her, but real love didn't vanish because a woman got angry with her lover.

Her lover. That's what he was, and that's what she was to him. God, he loved her. How could he have risked that love with even a tiny infraction? And no one could ever construe this morning's fiasco as a minor misstep.

Mitch paced Kim's living room, seeing none of its plush furnishings or stylish decor. He could hear the shower running; obviously she was doing more than "washing her face."

He couldn't stand it. She was in there acting as though they were mere acquaintances, keeping him waiting when he was hanging over an emotional cliff!

Throwing caution to the winds, Mitch went down the hall to Kim's bedroom and pushed the door open. She was just coming out of the bathroom, clad in a short blue robe. Her eyes narrowed menacingly. "I asked you to wait in the living room!"

"Don't get high-handed on me, Kim. If you're mad, say so. Yell at me, if you want. But don't issue orders and expect me to jump to obey."

She tossed her head back and walked to a dresser that had a round mirror over it. "If you came here to fight, you can just turn around and leave. I've had all of the misery I can handle for one summer."

Mitch moved closer. She was looking into the mirror, monkeying with her hair, attempting nonchalance and failing abysmally. But how could she be anything but tense? Wasn't there enough tension in his own body to support a suspension bridge? "I owe you an apology, and you have it. I also owe Sarge an apology—"

"It might be too late for apologies." Kim turned around.

"It's never too late if we love each other."

Kim's mouth thinned. "Getting an admission of love out of you was like pulling teeth."

"You're right. I was a fool about a lot of things, and not hog-tying and branding you the minute I set eyes on you was my biggest."

"Hog-tying and branding!" she scoffed. "Granted, I was about as easy as a woman can be, but I hardly think that macho attitude—"

Mitch cut in. "The only reason you were easy was because you fell so hard for me."

"Aren't we conceited today," Kim drawled.

"Is it a lie?" Mitch took another step forward. "Didn't you tell me that yourself? Didn't you say—?"

"Oh, stop it! Do you think I need a reminder of every fool thing I did with you?" She put on a disdainful expression. "I suppose you told Dad everything."

"Not everything, no. I don't think anyone has the right to know everything about us, do you?"

Kim looked away, haughtily. "That's not the point, anyway. You accused me of going back on my word. Your trust wouldn't cover the head of a pin, and I never gave you one single reason to mistrust me."

"No, you didn't. You were right—about everything—and I was wrong. What do you want me to do, take strychnine and die?"

Her eyes jerked back to his. "Don't be absurd!"

Mitch had to laugh. "Hey, I was only kidding. I might feel like the bottom of the barrel right now, but I don't intend to die over it."

Kim peered at him from beneath her lashes. "What... what did Dad say about us?"

Mitch shoved his hands into the pockets of his slacks. "That he wished one of us had told him what was going on."

"What did he say about your accusation? You did accuse him, like you did me, didn't you?"

"Almost point-blank," Mitch said with a guilty grimace. "He told me to either accept my own value to the company or to hit the road."

"Hit the road? He really said that?" Kim's eyes were wide and startled.

"Sarge doesn't mince words."

"Well, no, but..." Frowning, Kim leaned her hip against the dresser. "Are you out of a job now?"

"It's possible. He said to come back in the morning." Mitch shook his head. "I don't know what's going to happen, Kim. I screwed things up so royally, they're apt to never get back to normal."

"Why didn't you trust me?" she said in a quavery whisper, her eyes miserable. "Did someone hurt you so badly, you couldn't trust again?"

"No. There's no excuse for my behavior. Other than an almost obsessive desire to get ahead on my own. And I have no idea where that came from. My mother, sister and myself shared everything after my father died. We relied on each other every day of our life together. I'm blaming no one but myself for what I did. You have to understand that." He took another small step toward her. "Do you hate me?"

Her face colored. "Don't ask for feelings, Mitch. I'm not sure I have any to give right now."

"Other than anger."

"I'm not even angry now, just sort of empty," Kim said in a dull, defeated voice.

"I can make that go away," Mitch said softly. "You know I can." He moved close enough to put his hands on her waist.

She tried to wriggle out of his grasp. "That's not the answer!"

"It might be. Kim..." He tried to kiss her. "Kim...I love you."·

"Maybe I don't need your kind of love." But she was getting weak merely from his nearness. He smelled so good, and his hands gripping her waist were transferring his heat to her own body. "Mitch...don't. Please don't."

"Don't want you? Ask me to stop breathing, Kim. I could do that a lot easier."

"You didn't want me last night!"

"I was angry last night. Can't you forgive one stupid mistake? Kim, I swear I'll never mistrust you again. Look at me, honey." He let go with his right hand to tip her chin. "Look at me, Kim." Her eyes were brimming. "If you give me another chance, just one more chance, you'll never regret it. I'm begging, Kim. I'm ripping open my heart right now, exposing everything I am for you to see. I know how tightly I contained my feelings before, and it's something I'll regret to my dying day. But, baby, what we have is so special...."

Again he sought her lips, and this time he succeeded. Her mouth was partially open, and he drank in her breath and her taste and nearly melted from the sensation. He separated her robe and went inside it. Her skin was still slightly shower-damp, warm and soft and deliciously female. "Kim...oh, Kim." It was a groan, a plea, rising from the depths of his soul. She tried to ignore it, to fight it, but his physicality was overpowering her determination.

A groan built in her own throat. From the beginning she hadn't been able to resist Mitch, not even when it was her making the advances. Who had a better right to anger than she? Weren't mistrust and false accusations enough of a lesson for any woman? Why, then, was she so helpless in his arms?

"I don't want to forgive you," she whispered raggedly.

"I know, honey, I know." He trailed kisses from her lips to her throat, and down farther, to the swells of her breasts and the dewy skin in between. "You smell like no other woman," he whispered.

She knew precisely what he meant. Scent was so powerful in lovemaking, so crucial, and his was fogging her brain. He was seducing her mind as well as her body, making her want him with a staggering, overwhelming desire. He looked wonderful today, she realized dimly, dressed in slacks and a marvelous off-white shirt; clothes for the office. He'd probably left his coat and tie in the truck.

She was bent slightly backward so he could lavish kisses to her breasts. Her whole body was alive and tingling. Something joyful zinged through her vital organs. One so seldom found the perfect sexual mate; she never had until Mitch. Of course he could arouse her, seduce her with a few kisses and romantic caresses. It was natural for him—for them—for her—as natural as breathing. She sighed, resigned to loving him, however dim-wittedly he might behave on occasion. Besides, was any human being so saintly and self-controlled that he never lost touch with his own intelligence? Was she?

Mitch felt the change in her, the relaxing of her tension, the more yielding texture of her skin, her rising desire. She was sweetness and light, sin and seduction, the sun around which he revolved, his reason for living. She was woman—his woman, his love.

Overcome by emotion, he swept her off her feet and carried her to the unmade bed. There were tears in his eyes and he didn't care. Somehow tears seemed fitting. He was wide open, exposed and vulnerable, for the first time in his life completely steeped in love, saturated with it, so that no part of his body didn't feel it.

He lay over her, kissing her mouth, her cheeks, her eyelids. His voice was feverish and hoarse with emotion. "I've never felt like this before. I love you so much I can't express it. There are no words good enough, none strong enough to describe the fullness . . . the wonder. . . ."

It was how she had felt about him all along. She brought his head up to look into his misty eyes. "We're two very fortunate people, Mitch. Do you see that now?"

"Yes . . . yes." His lips descended to hers, and in seconds their moods had evolved from philosophical to lustful.

Kim began tearing at his clothes, her fingers awkward in her haste to unbutton his shirt and get rid of it. He helped, wriggling one way and then another to slither out of his pants and underwear. His shoes were kicked away. Somehow he managed to yank off his socks. Kim's robe vanished somewhere in the bedding. The pillows, top sheet and blanket, all askew, had been shaped into an intimate nest by their frantic gyrations to maintain caresses and kisses while they tossed Mitch's clothing.

It wasn't something either of them thought about. For that matter, thinking at all had nearly ceased for each of them. They had entered a world of sensation, where one exists solely for the next caress, the next kiss and the only goal was physical ecstasy. "I love you," was their theme song, their only words, and repetitiveness did not dull the litany's impact or import.

Kisses landed without direction, hungry kisses, needful kisses. Mitch spent delicious minutes in worshipful attention to her breasts, her belly, her thighs. Kim marveled at the symmetry of his chest and upper arms, absorbing the mysteries of his manhood through her fingertips. How she loved touching him! The incredible freedom of love admitted and exchanged had her flying. Today they were different with each other, on a lovely plane of togetherness, functioning as one entity, and the feeling was euphoric, the most desirable of human sensations.

They came together then, with a wildness that surpassed anything they'd previously known, as though some new, fierce flame had been ignited by controversy and forgiveness. She reveled in Mitch's weight, but then he rolled them both over and put her on top. "Sit up, baby," he whispered.

A heady smile curved her lips. Watching his face while she pleasured him was unbelievably exciting. He held her hips and directed the rhythm of their movements. She lifted, he lifted. She sank down on him, he groaned in supreme pleasure. She liked this position. Immensely.

Her hands splayed on his chest, and she bent forward to kiss his mouth. Her hair draped around both of them, a shroud of intimacy.

"You are one sexy man," she murmured against his lips. He chuckled, deep in his throat, a completely masculine sound, and in the next instant, he rolled them over again and she was flat on her back.

"As strong as... what's the name of that biblical muscle man?" she inquired.

"Samson? Hercules?"

"I don't think Hercules is in the Bible." Kim smiled serenely. "But he'll do." Her expression sobered. "I love your strength."

"What you love is my body, baby." He spoke gruffly though teasingly.

"First and foremost," she whispered. "But that's not all of it. I fell in love with *you*, Mitch, and you're much more than a gorgeous body." She laughed then, a husky run of notes. "On the other hand..." She was, after all, under him in the most erotic of situations, and it wasn't his mind making her giddy with lust.

He understood what she meant, and their spurt of conversation had gone on long enough. All traces of levity vanished from his expression. He kept his head up to see her eyes, while his thrusts became deeper, faster. Her lips parted. Her breath came quicker. They were approaching the crest, and he wanted to see the exact moment on her face.

She sucked in a breath and held it. "Mitch...oh, Mitch." Her eyes closed, opened briefly and closed again.

His own release overpowered all else. "Kim... *Kim!*"

Everything went silent, the creaking of the bed, the gasps and moans, the entire world. The only sounds within earshot, Kim realized vaguely, contentedly, were two hearts slowing down and two sets of lungs striving for oxygen.

She smiled, utterly replete, happier than she'd ever been.

But then her eyes opened, and she remembered what had brought Mitch here this morning.

"Mitch," she said softly. "I have to call my mother. Dad has probably spread the word by now, and I owe her an explanation. Him, too."

Mitch raised his head. "I have to talk to them, too."

"I'm glad you think so." Gently she caressed his face with her fingertips. "Should we do it together?"

He thought for a second, then kissed her and moved to the bed. "No, I don't think so. Talking to your folks is something I should do alone." Sitting up, he laid a hand on her cheek. "Is that all right with you?"

"I'm weighing what would be best," she murmured, thinking it through. Mitch had to make amends with her parents. She did, too, of course, but Sara and Sarge Armstrong should get to know the same Mitch she knew, and would that happen with her there? Wouldn't she worry and flutter and try to make everything all right? Probably no one else would get a word in, except her dad, that is. Sarge always got a word in, and sometimes that word wasn't particularly tactful.

"It's better for you to do it alone," she told Mitch. "I'll talk to Mother on the phone and then Dad. You do whatever it is you feel needs doing. On your own."

He nodded his agreement. "You realize there are no more secrets, Kim."

"It's best," she said gently.

"Before I start, there's something else that needs saying. I'm not sure I even have a job now, but will you marry me?"

Her eyes filled. "Yes."

"What if your folks never get over today?"

"They will, Mitch. They love me." She tried to laugh. "I'm not sure Dad will get over it enough to keep you on the payroll, but if he doesn't, we'll all live with it. My parents are very important to me, Mitch, and the one thing I couldn't abide is permanent discord with them."

"I understand."

Sitting up, Kim smiled bravely. "Well...shall we begin?"

"What do you want me to do, not mention our marriage plans, or tell them what's going on?"

"I . . . don't know. It could come up when I talk to them on the phone, couldn't it? What should I do, Mitch? What do you want me to do?"

Mitch made the decision. "I think you should tell them, but not until after I talk to them. How does that sound?"

Kim smiled. "Perfect. In fact, that's the one thing we should probably tell them together. Agreed?"

"Agreed."

Thirteen

After Mitch left, Kim sat down at the phone to make those calls to her parents. Sarge and Sara were reasonable people, and she wasn't worried about them forgiving and forgetting where she was concerned. Mitch, however, was another story. In retrospect, what he had done wasn't that terrible, but she was in love with him and her folks had no such emotional ties influencing their opinion.

Frowning, Kim gnawed her bottom lip. Mitch and her parents had to get along. Even as Mitch's wife she would be unhappy and at very loose ends if the three people she loved most never became friends. Mitch was on his way to make amends, and how would her talking to Sarge and Sara, before he had his day in court, help his case? This was something he had to do by himself, for himself, and heaven help them all if he struck out.

Slowly, thoughtfully, Kim picked up the phone and dialed her father's business number. The receptionist answered with the company name and Kim got right to the point. "Could I speak to Nan Houston, please?"

Nan came on the line. "Mr. Armstrong's office."

"Hello, Nan. This is Kim Armstrong. I'd like to leave a message for Dad."

Nan Houston was Sarge's secretary. "He's in a meeting right now, Kim, but I could break in."

"Please don't, Nan. Just give him a message when he's free. Tell him that I'll see him sometime this afternoon, all right?"

"Certainly, if that's what you prefer."

"Thanks, Nan. Goodbye."

Kim broke the connection and dialed her parents' home number. As usual, Lois answered. "Hi, Lois. Kim. Would you give Mother a message for me?"

"She's out in the rose garden, Kim. I can call her. Wouldn't take but a minute."

"That's not necessary. Just tell her I'll see her sometime today. She'll understand."

"Sure, Kim, no problem."

"Thanks, Lois. 'Bye."

Putting down the phone, Kim heaved a small sigh. But she felt better about her role in today's events, and got up to dress and begin her own day.

Mitch drove to his apartment for a change of clothes, then headed for the Armstrong building. The knot in his gut wasn't at all pleasant. Sarge might refuse to see him again today, or worse, throw him out on his ear. But if he did manage to see Kim's father and could convince Sarge to listen, then there was hope. It wasn't himself that Mitch was worried about anymore, it was Kim, and her relationship with her parents. He'd damaged something precious and important, and it was up to him to repair it.

He strode into the building and to the receptionist's desk. "Hello. I'm Mitch Conover and—"

The woman smiled. "I remember, Mr. Conover. You were here yesterday."

And early this morning, only the woman hadn't yet been at her desk. Mitch managed a weak smile. "Could you check with Mr. Armstrong and find out if I could have a few minutes with him?"

"I can check with his secretary." The woman picked up the phone and touched two numbers. "Nan? Mitch Conover is here and would like to see Mr. Armstrong." Mitch nervously shifted his weight. "Thanks, Nan." She put down the phone. "Mr. Armstrong is in a meeting, but it's almost over. You may wait, if you wish."

"Thank you." There were chairs nearby, and Mitch walked to one and sat down. What was he going to say to Sarge? More accurately, how best to say what had to be said? Marrying into a family was a big step for anyone, but causing a ruckus before the older generation even knew what was going on was starting pretty far down on the totem pole.

He tried hard to relax. Walking into Sarge's office with so much tension would hardly aid his cause. For the first time he really looked at the decor. Rich wood and colors, potted plants, undraped tinted windows. Kim's fine hand was in evidence.

It was fifteen minutes before the receptionist called, "You may go up now, Mr. Conover."

"Thanks." Mitch rose stiffly—there actually seemed to be a three-foot vise gripping the length of his spine—and walked to the elevator.

The second-floor hallway was carpeted, and his footsteps were barely discernible. Sarge's door was ajar. Mitch gingerly pushed it open. Sarge was standing at a window, his back to the door. Mitch cleared his throat.

Kim's father turned around. "Come in. And close the door."

"Yes, sir." Mitch moved closer to the desk, though Sarge remained near the window. "I know you said to come back in the morning, sir, but this really can't wait."

"Apparently not," Sarge said dryly. "Though," he added after a moment, "I never took you for an impetuous man."

"I'm not. Not usually. Most of the time I lean too far the other way."

"Oh? Are you saying you normally weigh decisions from every angle before implementing them?"

Mitch's face turned three shades of red. Obviously his actions of this summer had been weighed from only one angle: his. "Guess I don't know what I am," he mumbled. The defeat in that remark sunk in and he squared his shoulders. "That's not true. I know what I did and I know why I did it. My only defense is that I didn't expect things to come to this." The internal battles he'd waged over Kim raced through his mind, his numerous retreats and advances, her advances. There were aspects of their relationship he would never talk about with anyone, let alone with Sarge.

Sarge gestured to his desk and the chairs around it. "Let's sit down."

"Thanks." Mitch couldn't hide the relief he felt. At least Sarge was giving him a chance.

Settled, they looked across the desk at each other. "I've been thinking about the whole thing, Mitch, quite a lot. You didn't want to fall for Kim, did you?"

He thought before replying. "I didn't like the idea of a close friendship with the boss's daughter."

"Because I would make things easy for you." Sarge shook his head with a show of disgust. "You don't know me very well."

"There was more to it," Mitch said quietly. "I liked my job and believed I had a good chance of advancing in the company. I wanted to do it all on my own."

Sarge stared for a moment, then sat back. "Guess I can't fault that attitude. But your mistrust bothers me, and your having so little faith in your own ability. Are you lacking in self-confidence? You don't come across that way. Or, you didn't before this morning."

"I never thought about it," Mitch admitted. "Looking back, I can't see any other incidents where I behaved so...so..."

"Indecisively?"

"Stupidly." He leaned forward. "Sarge, if I've done permanent damage to your faith in Kim, I'll never forgive myself. That's why I'm here, to apologize for any problems I've caused between Kim and you." He looked down at the desk, ashamed, chagrined. "I intend to apologize to Mrs. Armstrong, too."

"I highly recommend that move," Sarge said with some dryness. "Incidentally, neither of us has heard a word from Kim about this."

Mitch's eyes jerked up. "She said she was going to call you both."

"Well, she hasn't." Sarge frowned. "Unless..." He picked up the phone. "Nan? Did my daughter call this morning? Thanks." He put down the phone. "Kim called while I was in a meeting. She said she'd be seeing me later today." Settling back into his chair, he regarded Mitch across the desk. "You two are serious, aren't you?"

Mitch nodded. "Very."

"Well, you can call this favoritism if you want—I call it good sense—but I can't fire my daughter's future husband." Sarge's craggy face softened. "Besides, you're still the man I want in this office."

Mitch's heart skipped a full beat before taking off into a wild rhythm. "I am?"

"You are. What d'ya say? Should we forget the whole thing and shake hands?"

"I'm willing." Willing? He'd like to leap up and do cartwheels on Sarge's carpet!

They stood up and solemnly shook hands over the desk. "Thank you, sir. You'll never regret it."

Sarge's grin was a yard wide. "I'll hold you to that, son."

Regardless of the elation in his system, Mitch approached the Armstrong's front door with his nerves jumping around. The woman he remembered as Lois answered. "Yes?"

"I'm Mitch Conover. Is Mrs. Armstrong at home?"

Lois looked him over. "You work for Mr. Armstrong, don't you?"

"Yes, ma'am."

"Wait here for a minute. I'll see if Mrs. Armstrong is receiving callers."

Mitch couldn't help grinning when the door closed in his face. Obviously Lois was a cautious woman. The door was opened a few minutes later by Sara Armstrong. "Hello, Mitch. Come in."

"Thank you, ma'am."

Sara brought him to the den. "Sit down."

Mitch tried to read her mood. Sara looked calm, no different than the other times he'd seen her. She was dressed nicely, wearing a tan cotton skirt and blouse and stylish shoes with a low heel. She smiled at him. "Sarge called only a minute ago and told me you'd be coming by."

"I came here directly from his office. Mrs. Armstrong . . ."

"Sara, please."

"I owe you an apology." Mitch looked down at his hands. "Kim and I . . ." He took a breath. "It's my fault she didn't say anything to you about seeing me, and I want you to know—"

"It's all right, Mitch. Don't be uncomfortable."

His eyes lifted. "Please don't hold it against Kim."

"I'm not upset with anyone, Mitch, and it would take much more than a little secrecy to harm my daughter's and my relationship." Sara smiled. "I knew she was involved with someone. I sensed it. For a time I thought it was Scot. You met Scot Taylor, didn't you?"

"Yes." He'd told Kim he wasn't jealous of Scot, but that had been little more than bluster. Taylor did, after all, seem like the perfect choice for a woman like Kim.

"Scot is engaged to be married," Sara said softly, apparently grasping the anxious expression on Mitch's face. "To a woman in California. Did you know that?"

"Uh . . . no." Was that relief he felt? He knew he had Kim's love, but he was glad he didn't have to compete with Taylor for her parents' affections. After all, the Armstrongs had probably hoped at one time that Taylor would become their son-in-law. "Kim didn't mention it."

"It probably never occurred to Kim that it mattered," Sara said gently. "I saw the lay of the land at the party, Mitch. Everything was suddenly quite clear."

"You're a perceptive woman."

"Where my daughter is concerned, yes," Sara agreed. "Kim's happiness is very important to her father and me. I'll tell you something in confidence, Mitch. Sarge and I wanted a large family, but because of some medical problems I had, Kim is our only child. Her husband will be the son we never had."

Mitch wanted to blurt it out. *We're going to be married. I'm going to be Kim's husband.* But he and Kim had agreed to relate the news together, and besides, from the warmth in Sara's eyes, she had already figured it out.

"Sarge told me about your new position in the company," Sara said then. "I couldn't be more pleased."

That old word rose up to taunt him, favoritism. But Sara's attitude wasn't Sarge's. If he hadn't been right for the job, Sarge never would have given it to him, regardless of Sarge's devotion to his daughter.

Mitch settled back. He was in love with the boss's daughter, planning to marry the boss's daughter. Those were facts, irrevocable, unchangeable. He would have fallen for Kim if she'd been an orphan, or her father had dug ditches for a living. He'd fallen in love with Kim, not with her position nor with her family.

But it was nice that she had such great parents. Their kids would have doting, loving grandparents. And with his own parents gone, the Armstrongs would be doubly important.

"Thanks for the vote of confidence," he replied to Sara, realizing at the same moment that for the first time he felt completely at ease with her. Everything was great, almost unbelievably so.

They talked for an hour before Mitch got up to leave. "I have to see Kim."

"Yes, of course." Sara offered her hand, then bypassed the formality for a hug. "Welcome to the family, Mitch."

He smiled all over his face. "Thanks, Sara."

* * *

"And then she asked us for dinner tonight. I told her we'd be there. I hope that's all right with you." Mitch's detailed accounting of the day's events had been recited on his feet, as there was too much excitement broiling within him to sit.

Kim had listened with glistening, joyful eyes. At one point she felt an urge to say, "I told you so," but thank goodness she managed to stifle that destructive impulse. "It's very right with me, Mitch." He was so handsome pacing the floor, destroying any semblance of neatness in his thick dark hair with runs of his fingers, stopping periodically to look at her with glowing, shining eyes.

He stopped now. She'd been leaning against the kitchen counter, and he placed his hands on her waist and pulled her forward. "We can tell them about our plans tonight, Kim."

"A perfect time," she agreed. Tenderly she touched his face. "Are you happy, Mitch?"

Emotion played across his face. "There aren't words to describe how happy."

"Me, too," she whispered, and cuddled against his body with a contented sigh. "What if I hadn't sent you that invitation from Meridian Homes?"

Mitch kissed the top of her head. "Thank God you're a persistent lady."

Kim laughed softly. "That's a kindly way of putting it, darling. I chased you shamelessly." When he didn't answer, she tilted her head to see his face. "Didn't I?"

A teasing grin touched his mouth. "Let's put it another way. You chased me till I caught you. How's that?"

Kim's laughter rang out. "It's wonderful. Very tactful." Her expression sobered. "I've never really believed in happily ever after, but I think in our case it's a distinct possibility. Mitch, will you promise me something?"

"Anything, honey. Just name it."

"Will you always talk to me?"

"I don't understand."

"About anything. About your day, and mine. About my faults, and yours. About feelings, especially hurt feelings. I believe in that old theory of never letting the sun set on a quarrel.''

''We're not going to quarrel, Kim.'' He cocked an eyebrow. ''Are we?''

Kim's features took on a devilish cast. ''If we do, I'll chase you around the house until you catch me.'' She snuggled closer. ''How about catching me right now? We have an hour before we have to get ready for dinner.''

His hands slid down to her bottom. ''An hour should do it, honey. Yes, I think an hour is just time enough.''

''Prove it,'' she whispered, lifting her lips to his.

He proved it just fine.

* * * * *

COMING NEXT MONTH

Take 4 bestselling love stories FREE

Plus get a FREE surprise gift!

Special Limited-time Offer

Mail to Silhouette Reader Service™

3010 Walden Avenue
P.O. Box 1867
Buffalo, N.Y. 14269-1867

YES! Please send me 4 free Silhouette Desire® novels and my free surprise gift. Then send me 6 brand-new novels every month, which I will receive months before they appear in bookstores. Bill me at the low price of $2.44 each plus 25¢ delivery and applicable sales tax, if any.* That's the complete price and a savings of over 10% off the cover prices—quite a bargain! I understand that accepting the books and gift places me under no obligation ever to buy any books. I can always return a shipment and cancel at any time. Even if I never buy another book from Silhouette, the 4 free books and the surprise gift are mine to keep forever.

225 BPA ANRS

Name	(PLEASE PRINT)
Address	Apt. No.
City	State	Zip

This offer is limited to one order per household and not valid to present Silhouette Desire® subscribers. *Terms and prices are subject to change without notice.
Sales tax applicable in N.Y.

UDES-295

©1990 Harlequin Enterprises Limited

He's Too Hot To Handle...but she can take a little heat.

This summer don't be left in the cold, join
Silhouette for the hottest Summer Sizzlers collection.
The perfect summer read, on the beach or while
vacationing, Summer Sizzlers features sexy heroes
who are "Too Hot To Handle." This collection of
three new stories is written by bestselling authors
Mary Lynn Baxter, Ann Major and Laura Parker.

Available this July wherever
Silhouette books are sold.

SS95

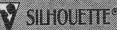

SILHOUETTE®

of the

Month

1995

Here are the men you've been waiting for all your life—*hotter* than you ever imagined in your wildest dreams!

They're created by the top authors in contemporary romance—the ones *you* say again and again are your favorites...

In July
THE DISOBEDIENT BRIDE
by Joan Johnston

In August
THE WILDE BUNCH
by Barbara Boswell

In September
ALEX AND THE ANGEL
by Dixie Browning

In October
WILDCAT
by *New York Times* bestselling author
Rebecca Brandewyne

In November
ANGELS AND ELVES
by Joan Elliott Pickart

In December
A COWBOY CHRISTMAS
by Ann Major

Man of the Month...only from Silhouette Desire

MOM95JD

COMING IN JULY FROM

SILHOUETTE®

Desire®

THE DISOBEDIENT BRIDE
by Joan Johnston

book three of her bestselling

CHILDREN OF

HAWK'S WAY

series

Texas rancher Zach Whitelaw advertised for a wife to bear his children—but if she wasn't pregnant in a year's time, he'd divorce her! Six months into their marriage, Rebecca Littlewolf Whitelaw's tummy was as flat as on her wedding day. So, short of stuffing a pillow under her shirt, what was a wife in love supposed to do?

Don't miss THE DISOBEDIENT BRIDE in July...only from Silhouette Desire.

SDHW7

In June, get ready for thrilling romances and FREE BOOKS—Western-style— with...

WESTERN *Lovers*

You can receive the first 2 Western Lovers titles FREE!

June 1995 brings Harlequin and Silhouette's WESTERN LOVERS series, which combines larger-than-life love stories set in the American West! And WESTERN LOVERS brings you stories with your favorite themes... "Ranch Rogues," "Hitched In Haste," "Ranchin' Dads," "Reunited Hearts" the packaging on each book highlights the popular theme found in each WESTERN LOVERS story!

And in June, when you buy either of the Men Made In America titles, you will receive a WESTERN LOVERS title absolutely FREE! Look for these fabulous combinations:

♦ Buy ALL IN THE FAMILY
by Heather Graham Pozzessere (Men Made In America) and receive a FREE copy of BETRAYED BY LOVE by Diana Palmer (Western Lovers)

♦ Buy THE WAITING GAME
by Jayne Ann Krentz (Men Made In America) and receive a FREE copy of IN A CLASS BY HIMSELF by JoAnn Ross (Western Lovers)

Look for the special, extra-value shrink-wrapped packages at your favorite retail outlet!

HARLEQUIN®   Silhouette®

WL-T

Announcing
the New **Pages & Privileges**™ Program
from Harlequin® and Silhouette®

Get All This FREE
With Just One Proof-of-Purchase!

- **FREE Hotel Discounts** of up to 60% off at leading hotels in the U.S., Canada and Europe

- **FREE Travel Service** with the guaranteed lowest available airfares plus 5% cash back on every ticket

- **FREE $25 Travel Voucher** to use on any ticket on any airline booked through our Travel Service

- **FREE Petite Parfumerie** collection (a $50 Retail value)

- **FREE Insider Tips Letter** full of fascinating information and hot sneak previews of upcoming books

- **FREE Mystery Gift** (if you enroll before June 15/95)

And there are more great gifts and benefits to come!
Enroll today and become Privileged!

(see insert for details)

PROOF-OF-PURCHASE

Offer expires October 31, 1996

SD-PP2